哈福

美國口語
一週通

American
Talks Made Easy

附
MP3

施孝昌 · Charles Krohn 合著

哈福

【前言】　用國中英語
就能和外國人聊不停

　　英語真的很難嗎？其實，發現一本能教你活學活用英語的書才難。本書正是要教你如何憑國中英語與老外對答如流。

　　每一位華人，如果只算中學時代，英文課最少上了一千五百六十小時，自習時間最少二千一百九十小時。如以每天上班八小時來計算，每週四十四小時，這樣的時間約合一年八個月的工作時間。

　　依您現在的薪水，請問您已投資多少錢在學習英語？這樣的努力和投資，能有幾人可以用英語約老外出去？可以跟商人討價還價？這時候除了 angry 和 happy 兩個字之外，有幾人可以用英語確切表達出自己的喜怒哀樂？如果這樣想，英語真的很難！

　　不過，英語真的很難嗎？那為什麼美國白癡也會講英語？

　　其實，你應該會的英語，中學早已學過！來！測試一下。下列的句子，您不用花時間去翻譯成連美國人也聽不懂的洋涇濱，請按句尾指示的章節去看看您是不是每個字都已學過：

1. 我先生認為我好像什麼都不會。我一點也沒有決定權。
   （UNIT 42 情況會話）

2. 前幾天我回家太晚，老爸對我暴跳如雷。
   （UNIT 46 情況會話）

3. 這個價錢已經最低，不能再減價了。
   （UNIT 34 相關語彙）

4. 我對數學滿頭霧水。（UNIT 15 情況會話）

5. 林小姐很平易近人。（UNIT 5 情況會話）

　　本書是美國 AA BRIDGERS 公司，以最科學的方法，為華人和亞洲語系人士編寫的一系列飛越廿一世紀的英語學習工具書之一。

　　全書以最簡單的英語用字，每日一句口語的方法，來擴張您的英語話題。本書的話題涵蓋上班、學校、交遊、政治、經濟、名人勵志等。

　　全書共計 8500 字次，其中單音節字 7000 次，雙音節字 800 次，三音節字只有 250 次。

　　用這些簡單的字，組成共一千種句型、語法和應答。依據佛來茜分析法，小學六年級以上程度都可以學習。

　　本書裡任何一個句型和語法都可現學現用。48 個UNIT，每個都附有簡便記憶法，讓您一看就一輩子記得，不會再忘記。

　　另外，本書附有 MP3，如同老朋友間使用英語聊天的方法，輕輕鬆鬆就可增進您的聽力和記憶。

　　活用已經學過的單字片語，就可增進許多新的會話能力。如果您過去花了很多時間背單字、記文法，卻效果不彰，不妨跟著本書和所有 AA BRIDGERS 系列，您會發現，英語對您其實不難！

CONTENTS
目錄

PART II

PART III

PART IV

PART I

UNIT 1

GIVE ME A BREAK!
（你得了吧！你算了吧！）

說明

這句話就是台語「嗤你嘛好啊！」的意思。

人是奇怪的動物，根據美國統計，一個人每天說過的話，有三百句以上是口是心非。每天與你來往的人，不管他們是有意、無意、善意、惡意，總有幾百句謊言、藉口、偽善要傳到你耳朵。很煩，是不是？給他來句 GIVE ME A BREAK 吧！

【情況會話 1】 *********************

(John 和 Julie 約會，大小姐遲到了，嘴裡總要找理由。)

Julie: Sorry for coming late, John. I couldn't catch a taxi because of the rain.
（抱歉來晚了。下雨嘛！人家搭不上計程車。）

John: Oh, give me a break. You are TWO hours late.

（得了吧！妳遲到兩小時啦！）

　　break 是斷掉的意思。引申為一段一段之間，段落休息的意思。give me a break! 也就是你可以停止，讓我耳根子休息休息吧。

【 相關語彙 】

▶ **sorry for something:** 為某件事抱歉，注意用介係詞 for，後面要用名詞或動名詞。

　　例 Sorry for the trouble.
　　（給你添麻煩，不好意思。）

▶ **catch a taxi:** 搭上計程車

▶ **take a taxi:** 搭計程車

　　例 I wanted to take a taxi, but I couldn't catch one.
　　（我想搭計程車，但搭不上。）

▶ **because of:** 由於某種原因的意思。本句介係詞用 of。

【情況會話 2】 ***************

(約翰和茱莉這對男女朋友在一起談心，約翰不知趣地自哀自怨。)

John: Somehow, I am not happy.
（總之，我不快樂。）

Julie: Wait a minute, John. You've got a good job. You have a nice girlfriend like me, and you are not happy? Give me a break.
（什麼？約翰，你的工作不錯，又有個像我這麼好的女朋友，你還不快樂？得了吧！）

【相關語彙】

▸ **somehow:** some 是某種，how 是怎麼。兩個字加在一起有「不知為什麼，反正、總之」的意思。

例 Somehow, we've got to do it.
（不管什麼方法，總之，我們得做。）

▸ **wait a minute:** 原意是等一下。注意聽 MP3，把 wait 聲音拉長，minute 聲音放低，就變成不敢置信，「什麼話」的意思。

例 Wait a minute. Are you saying she is not coming?
（什麼？你是說她不來了？）

【情況會話 3】 *******************

(John 和主管在會議中的一段話。)

John: If you give me some more time, I can get it done better.
(要是你能給我多一點時間，我可以做得更好。)

Boss: Give me a break, John. It's your job to get things done better in the first place.
(算了吧，約翰！你本來就該一開始時就把事情做得很好。)

【相關語彙】

▶ **get something done better:** 把事情做得更好

例 Let me give you two more weeks, I hope you'll get it done better.
(我再給你兩星期時間，希望你把它做得更好。)

▶ **in the first place:** 一開始；剛開始

例 You shoud have let me know in the first place.
(你一開始就應該告訴我。)

UNIT 2

PUT ON AIRS

（擺架子）

說明

這句話就是台語「臭屁」的意思。

優越感是促使文明進步的原動力，所以人們往往喜歡擺上一付架子。想想看，我們日常對人品足論道，是不是常說別人愛臭屁呢？英語叫 put on airs.

【情況會話 1】

****

(茱莉和約翰在談論 Jenny。)

Julie: Jenny is always acting like she is a queen or something. I don't like it.
（珍妮老是裝得像皇后一樣，我不喜歡。）

John: Me, neither. She likes to put on airs too much.
（我也不喜歡。她太愛擺架子了。）

put on 是穿上衣服的意思。air 是空氣,加上 s 表示一種氣勢。所以 put on airs 就是擺一付架子。通常指裝模作樣,是反面的批評。

【相關語彙】

▶ **act like:** 裝得像什麼似的。like 是介係詞,像的意思。

例 You are a student. You've got to act like a student.
(你是個學生,就要有學生的樣子。)

▶ **Me, either.:** 我也不。在美國口語上,either 也可以用 neither 代替,叫 Me, neither. 或 Me, too. 是「我也是」或「我也要─」的意思。參照下一個單元。

【情況會話 2】

****

(這回,約翰和茱莉評論的是辦公室新來的女秘書。)

Julie: I hate the secretary in my office. She is always putting on airs like she is from the royal family.
(我討厭新來的秘書。她老愛擺一付臭架子,好像自己是貴族一般。)

John: Come on, give her some time. She is new. She will change.

（好了好了，給她一些時間。新來的嘛，以後會改的啦。）

【相關語彙】

▶ **I hate something or someone:** hate 未必是痛恨的意思，一般頂多是討厭罷了。注意：hate 是及物動詞，後面要是接「事情」，若是動詞要改成動名詞。

例 I hate smoking.
（我最不喜歡抽煙。）

I hate people smoking.
（我最討厭別人抽煙。）

▶ **come on:** 是一種口頭禪，表示要開始說話或做事，有好了好了的意思。

例 Come on, let's go.
（好了，走吧！）

ME, EITHER.
（我也不是，我也不要。）

說明

　　一天裡總要說上幾回「我也要」或「我也不要」之類的話。畢竟跟著別人後面做同樣的意見或選擇最是安全，又可以表示與朋友共進退的義氣，聰明人是不可以不知道這兩句話的英語叫 Me, too. 和 Me, either.。

【情況會話 1】 *******************

(談國家現況)

Julie: I am not sure the whole country is going to the right direction.
（我不曉得整個國家的方向，對還是不對。）

John: Me, either. But who cares?
（我也不曉得，可是，管他的。）

▶ **the right direction:** 正確方向

例 Are you sure this is the right direction?
（你確定這是正確方向？）

▶ **Who cares?:** 管他去的。

例 A: You can't smoke here.
（你不能在這兒抽煙。）

B: Who cares?
（管他去的。）

【情況會話 2】 **********************

（出門之前）

Julie: Forget about the umbrella, I don't think it's gonna rain.
（不用帶傘了。我想不會下雨。）

John: Me, either. But I'll still take it with me, just in case.
（我想也不會。不過，我還是帶著以防萬一。）

【相關語彙】

▶ **forget about something:** 不要管某種東西了。

例 Forget about her. She is not coming.
（別理她了。她不會來了。）

▶ **just in case:** 萬一。

例 Let's leave a message for her, just in case she comes.
（我們留個話給她，萬一她來了 [可以看見]）。

▶ **is gonna:** 美國人喜歡用 is going to 來表示就要，或將來會如何，可是他們不愛一字一句地說，經常很快地說成 is gonna。

例 Is she gonna come?
（她要來嗎？）

I am gonna do it myself.
（我要親自做。）

UNIT 4

GET THE GREEN LIGHT
（得到許可；獲准）

說明

英語就是這麼簡單，不要嘗試背太多冷門生澀的單字，使自己產生嚴重的挫折感，錯怪自己的記憶力，以為自己馬上記、馬上忘。其實，用最簡單的字，最富生活意味的詞來表達一個意思，大家聽起來親切，又容易懂。像本句 get the green light，只要走過十字路口，知道綠燈可以通行的人，哪有記不住這句話的？

【情況會話 1】　*********************

（朋友約好時間，Denny 卻還不見人影。）

John:　Denny may not be coming. He is late.
Almost twenty minutes late.
（丹尼大概不會來了。他遲到都快二十分鐘了。）

20

Julie: He probably couldn't get the green light to come.

(也許他得不到許可出門。[父母不准吧？])

get 是得到，the green light 指綠燈通行。get the green light 就是得到准許做什麼事。

【相關語彙】

▶ **may be:** 可能是某種狀況，be 是動詞。

▶ **maybe:** may 和 be 兩個字有時連在一起，當成一個副詞，與 probably 相同。也是或許的意思。

例 A: Take the umbrella. Maybe it will rain.
(帶著傘吧，或許會下雨。)

B: Yes, it may be raining.
(是啊，也許會下雨。)

【情況會話 2】   *********************

(顧客對秘書提出要求。)

Visitor: Can you show me the file?
(你可不可以讓我看看檔案？)

Secretary: Sorry. I can't do that before I get the green light.

（對不起。沒得到允許之前，我不能那樣做。）

【相關語彙】

▶ **can you show me:** 可不可以讓我看看 ....，購物或問路時最常用。

例 Can you show me the red one, please.
（能不能請你拿紅色那一個給我看看？）

Can you show me the way to the restroom?
（能不能告訴我廁所在那裡？）

【情況會話 3】 ********************

（媽媽在家裡抱怨爸爸。）

Mama: You are going to spoil the child. How could you let him go out without giving him the green light first?

（你會把孩子寵壞！你怎麼讓他沒得到允許之前就出去了？）

Daddy: O.K. Next time I'll have him check with you.

（好，下回我讓他先問妳。[可以了吧？]）

【相關語彙】

▶ **spoil:** 弄壞、糟蹋

例 We were having a good game when the rain came and spoiled it.
(我們比賽正起勁的時候就下雨了，糟蹋我們的比賽。)

▶ **How could you....?:** 你怎麼可以 ....，埋怨別人時候專用。

例 How could you use my car without asking me first?
(你怎麼可以不先問我就用我的車？)

▶ **have someone do somethihg:** 叫某人做某件事。人之後的動詞用原形就可以。

例 I'll have him come to see you.
(我會叫他來見你。)

▶ **check with someone:** check 是查的意思。本句是查詢。

例 We checked with the teacher. There will be no test tommorrow.
(我們問過老師了，明天沒考試。)

UNIT 5

DOWN TO EARTH; (DOWN-TO-EARTH)
（平易近人，不擺架子）

說明

　　人際關係很重要，所以在人類語言裡，有關人的個性語句也很多，偏偏英文教科書中，這種字句都很缺乏，不但學不到 put on airs，就是要說一個人非常容易相處也不知如何開口。其實這些字您早學過。老師「忘」了告訴您而已。

【情況會話 1】 ＊＊＊＊＊＊＊＊＊＊＊＊＊＊＊＊＊＊＊＊＊

（辦公室裡的悄悄話）

Juile: What do you think of our new boss?
（你對我們的新上司，印象如何？）

John: He is O.K. He seems to be a real down-to-earth person.

（他還好啦。他看起來似乎很平易近人。）

> 我們說神仙是高高在上。那麼相對的，神仙下凡來到地球 down to earth 就跟你我一樣平起平坐，當然平易近人了。

【相關語彙】

▸ **What do you think of....?:** 你覺得（印象）如何？

例 What do you think of the Chinese team? Are they going to win?
（您覺得中華隊怎樣？會贏嗎？）

▸ **He is O.K.:** 他還好。這句話可以指馬馬虎虎過得去，也可用在有人摔跤意外而沒受傷時。

▸ **real:** 美國口語中，用 real 比用 very 多，兩個意思一樣。別把它想成「真的」。

例 I am real happy with my job.
（我對我的工作很滿意。）

【情況會話 2】 *********************

(辦公室裡，新老闆約見茱莉。)

Boss: My door is always open. Feel free to see me any time.
(我的門永遠是開著的，有事隨時來見我。)

Julie: I will. I understand you are very down to earth.
(我會的，我知道你很平易近人。)

【相關語彙】

▶ **My door is always open.:** 當主管一定要熟記這句話，表示開明。我的門永遠是開著的。

▶ **feel free to:** 隨時。用在說話或寫信的最後一句。

例 If you have any questions, feel free to call me at 122-3331.
(有問題的話，隨時打電話到 122-3331 給我。)

▶ I will: 我會。當別人叮囑你做事，你可以用本句回答，簡單扼要。

例 A: Be sure to stop by if you are in town.
([有機會] 到本市，一定要來我家。)

B: Yes, I will.
(我會的。)

【情況會話 3】 *******************

(John 和 Julie 在閒聊)

Julie:　Miss Lin is very down to earth.
　　　　（ 林小姐很隨和。）

John:　I think so, too.
　　　　（ 我也這麼想。）

【相關語彙 】

▶ **I think so, too.:** 我同意、我有同感的意思。當別人敘述一個意見，你可以用本句表示相同看法。

　　例 A:　I think it's gonna rain.
　　　　　（ 我看會下雨噢。）

　　　　B:　I think so, too.
　　　　　（ 我想也是。）

▶ **I think so.:** 跟上句不同的是，本句沒有 too，這是用在別人問你意見的時候。

　　例 A:　Do you think it's going to rain?
　　　　　（ 你看會不會下雨呢？）

　　　　B:　Yes, I think so.
　　　　　（ 我想會吧 !）

UNIT 6

WALK ON A THIN ICE
（戰戰兢兢；如履薄冰；小心翼翼）

說明

　　華人用到本句的機會最多了，因為我們的父母，上司一般都比較保護年輕人，往往叮嚀再叮嚀，要我們凡事 walk on a thin ice。

【情況會話 1】 *********************

（做事之前，約翰叮嚀茱莉。）

John: We've got to be as careful as walking on a thin ice. We can't afford to make a mistake.
（我們必須小心翼翼，我們可犯不起錯誤。）

Julie: Yes, we've got to.
（是啊，我們得小心。）

　　本句的語法，就是走在薄薄的冰上面。不過 walk 雖然是「走」的意思，一般不會用在 He walks on a thin ice. 的句子裡，因為這樣就沒有比喻小心**翼翼**的意思；一般都用在 as 或 like 的後面，表示「像」走在薄冰上而已。注意 walk 直接加在這兩字後面，要用 walking 的形式。

【相關語彙】

▶ **have got to:** 必須。在美國口語中除非要強調別無選擇，否則一般不單用 have to 而用 have got to，並且把 have 與前面的人稱合說成 've got to。很多華人都聽不出有 've 的聲音，而只說 got to 是不對的。

例 We've got to get going.
（我們得走了。）

例 You've got to tell me if you are coming or not.
（你一定得告訴我你來還是不來。）

▶ **can't afford to:** 經不起（風險或打擊）；付不起（錢）

例 I can't afford to buy a car now.
（我現在買不起車子。）

例 We can't afford to lose the business.
（我們可經不起失去這筆生意。）

▶ **make a mistake:** 犯錯誤。

例 I made a mistake in my math problem.
（我數學題裡犯了一個錯誤。）

【情況會話 2】 ************************

（約翰和茱莉在談論丹尼的做事方式。）

John: Whatever Denny is doing, he is always
acting like he is walking on a thin ice.
（不論丹尼做什麼事，他都表現得小心翼翼。）

Julie: There is nothing wrong to be cautious.
（謹慎一點總不會錯的。）

【相關語彙】

▶ **Whatever:** 不管是什麼

例 Whatever you do, try your best.
（不管你做什麼事，[總得] 盡全力去做。）

▶ **There is nothing wrong to:** 做某件事，沒什麼不
對

例 There is nothing wrong to get up a little
late on Sunday.
（星期天晚一點起床沒什麼不對。）

▶ **cautious:** 謹慎。比 careful 語氣強。有警示的涵意。

例 You've got to be very cautious when driving in Taipei.
(在台北開車，一定要很小心謹慎。)

【情況會話 3】 ＊＊＊＊＊＊＊＊＊＊＊＊＊＊＊＊＊＊＊＊＊

(約翰在抱怨媽媽。)

John: I can't stand my Mom. She wants me to handle things like walking on a thin ice.
(我受不了我老媽，她老叫我要戰戰兢兢做事。)

Julie: Your Mom is right. You can't be too careful.
(令堂是對的，你小心一點總不過分。)

【相關語彙】

▶ **I can't stand:** 受不了。後面要名詞，人或事物。

例 I can't stand the heat. Give me some ice water, please.
(我受不了這種熱，請給我一點冰水。)

例 I can't stand you any longer. Please go away.
(我再也受不了你了，請走吧。)

▶ **can't be too:** 再怎麼樣也不算過分。強調一定要怎樣的意思，後面要加形容詞。

例 You can't be too nice to your parents.
（你對父母本來就應該很好。）

can't 的後面，也可以用動詞，而不用 be，這時記得 too 後面用副詞。

例 A good student can't study too hard.
（好學生本來就該認真讀書。）

A good employee can't work too hard.
（好夥計本來就該用心工作。）

UNIT 7

MP3-8

DRAW A LINE BETWEEN
（分辨；認清）

說明

　　雖然有不同的說法可以表達分辨的意思，但含意各有不同。學校英語中常學到 tell A from B，分別 A 和 B。它強調的是方法上的分辨，A 與 B 之間可以沒有任何相關性質。但在口語上，經常講的是對比性的分辨，或性質相近足以混淆的事物，如善惡、是非等。這種分辨的說法，就非 draw a line between 莫屬了。

【情況會話 1】 *********************

(Julie 很不滿意 John 搞錯了酒。)

Julie: Beer is not what I want. Can't you draw a line between wine and beer?
（啤酒不是我要的，難道你不會分辨酒和啤酒啊？）

John: All right, I would get some for you. You really drive me up the wall.
（好了，我去弄一些給你，妳真把我弄瘋了。）

　　draw a line 是畫線的意思，bwtween 是在兩者之間。所以在兩者之間畫線就是界定、弄清兩者含意的意思，用在分辨對比性或同性質不同含意的東西上。

【相關語彙】

▶ **not what I want:** 不是我要的。

　　例 Words are not what I want. What I want is action.
　　（我要的不是空話而已，我要的是行動。）

▶ **drive me up the wall:** 把我逼瘋了。（請參閱下個單元。）

【情況會話 2】 ********************

(媽媽對兒子的叮嚀。)

Mom: It's very important to be able to draw a line between good and bad. Stop hanging out with those kids.

(分辨好壞是很重要的，別老跟那些小鬼在一起瞎混。)

Son: You've said that a thousand times, Mom. Don't you ever think I am old enough to take care of myself?
(媽，妳說了一千次了，妳從沒想過我已大到可以照顧自己了嗎？)

【相關語彙】

▶ **stop Ving:** (Ving 是動詞加 ing 的意思)。停止動作，不要再做的意思。

例 Stop smoking. It's not good to your health.
(不要再抽煙了，對健康不好。)

▶ **hang out with:** 跟某些人在外面廝混。

例 The reason I hang out with Mr. Lin so much is because he can bring a lot of business to us.
(我之所以常跟林先生在外面廝混，是因為他可以給我們帶來很多生意。)

▶ **Don't you ever....?:** 從來沒有嗎？

例 Don't you ever shop at Sogo?
(你從來沒有在 Sogo 百貨購物嗎？)

DRIVE SOMEONE UP THE WALL

（把人逼得快瘋了。）

說明

有時候，人難免心裡煩。當你心裡很煩，卻偏偏有人不知趣，一而再再而三地要你做這做那，當你被他弄得火大了，有必要讓對方知道心裡的不高興，就說 You rive me up the wall.(我被你給逼瘋了)。

【情況會話 1】 ********************

(小兒子 John 一整天吵個不停，老爸受不了啦，對老媽說 ....。)

Dad: John is driving me up the wall. Would you please keep him quiet.

（約翰真要把我逼瘋了，請妳叫他安靜點好嗎？）

Mom:　　All right, I'll take him away.
　　　　　（好啦！我把他帶開。）

　　drive 原意是駕駛，當後面接的是人的時候就是驅
使之意。up the wall 是跳到牆上。drive someone up the
wall，就是把人逼到受不了，連牆都要爬上去，只求能
避開，當然就快要被逼瘋了。

【相關語彙】

▶ **keep someone quiet:** 叫某人安靜點。

　例　Please keep everybody quiet, the President
　　　is making the speech.
　　　（請讓大家保持安靜，總統就要開始講話了。）

▶ **take someone or something away:** 把人或東西
帶走

　例　The bank takes John's car away because he
　　　fails to make payments.
　　　（銀行把約翰的車子弄走，因為他沒有付錢。）

【情況會話 2】 *******************

(John 和 Julie 談論著數學老師。)

John: You know what? Our math teacher is really driving me up the wall with all these never-ending tests.
（妳知道嗎？我們數學老師那一連串永遠考不完的試，快要把我弄瘋了。）

Julie: I hear you. But he is not the only teacher doing that.
（我同情你，可是也不止他一個老師這樣。）

【相關語彙】

▶ **You know what?** 你知道嗎？這不是真正要問人家問題，只是個開場白而已。

例 You know what? If you want to make money in the stock market of Taiwan, forget about what you have learned in business school.
（你知道嗎？如果你想在台灣股市賺錢，商學院裡學的那一套要先忘掉。）

▶ **never-ending:** 永無止境的

例 A mother's love to her children is never-ending.
（母親對孩子的愛是永無止境的。）

▶ **I hear you:** 我同情你。當別人說了一件事，你表示同情地說「是啊」的意思。

【情況會話 3】 ********************

(John 很興奮地告訴 Julie。)

John:　Hey, Julie. You want to hear about my new girlfriend?
（嗨，茱莉。要不要聽我新女朋友的事？）

Julie:　Cut it out, John. Your story will drive me up the wall. You know that.
（省省吧，約翰。你知道你那些故事會叫我發瘋。）

【相關語彙】

▶ **cut it out:** 不要再說、省省口舌。當別人說的話你不愛聽，叫他 cut it out.

例 A:　How about going to a dinner on Saturday night.
（星期六晚上一起吃飯如何？）

B:　Cut it out. I am not going.
（不要再說了，我不去。）

▶ **You know that:** 你清楚得很。

例 I am not going to dinner with you. You know that.
（我不會與你去吃飯的，你清楚得很。）

UNIT 9

MP3-10

BEAT SOMEONE UP
（好好揍一頓，徹頭徹尾地打敗。）

說明

這句話就是台語的「[乎你] 一頓粗飽粗飽」。

美國口語中最普遍的一句。華人平日也經常用得到，英語卻不知道如何表達才能顯出這種絕對的憤怒和挫折，其實就是 beat up 這麼簡單。

【情況會話 1】 ********************

(有人把 John 的書撕成碎片。)

John: I'll find out who did it and I am going to beat him up real bad.
（我一定要找出是誰幹的，我會好好地痛揍他一頓。）

Julie: That won't solve anything. Come on, let me help you pick up the pieces.
（那於事無補。來吧，我幫你把碎片撿起來。）

> beat 是一下接一下打的意思。好像音樂的拍子或心跳都是 beat。up 在美語中有完完全全的意思。beat 和 up 二字連起來，就是好好揍一頓。若是被動式，被人家好好地 beatten up，就是被打慘了、在比賽中輸慘了。

【相關語彙】

▶ **find out:** 找出來；發現

例 I can't wait to find out who the winner will be.
(我等不及知道誰會是得獎人。)

▶ **that won't solve anything:** 那解決不了什麼事。

例 Stop crying. That won't solve anything.
(不要哭了，那解決不了什麼事。)

▶ **pick up:** 撿起來；接人；挑一個。

例 What's on the floor? Would you please pick it up?
(地上是什麼東西，請你撿起來好嗎？)

例 I've got to pick up my wife at the airport.
(我得到機場接我太太。)

囫 I have several books here. Pick one up for yourself.
（我有幾本書在這裡，你自己挑一本吧。）

【情況會話 2】 ***********************

（兩個球迷在對話。）

John: I can't believe they could be beaten up so
bad.
（真難相信他們竟然輸得那麼慘。）

Julie: Well, they have done everything they can.
I hope next game they will win.
（他們已經盡力而為。希望下一場他們會贏。）

【相關語彙】

▶ **I can't believe:** 我真不敢相信。後面接句子。

囫 I can't believe people are so crazy about
Michael Jackson.
（我真不敢相信大家對麥克傑可遜那樣瘋狂。）

▶ **do everything someone can:** 盡某人之力而為。

囫 The police are doing everything they can
stop crime.
（警方盡其所能地防止犯罪。）

【情況會話 3】 ********************

(John 和 Julie 的朋友 Frank 心情很差。)

John: Frank is so down these days. It seems he's been totally beaten up.

（法蘭克這幾天沮喪得很，好像鬥敗的公雞一樣。）

Julie: I think so, too. Maybe we ought to do something to help him.

（我也這麼認為。或許我們該做點事幫幫他。）

【相關語彙】

▶ **so down:** 美語用字實在很簡單，講人的心情鬱悶到極點，垂頭喪氣叫 so down。

例 I don't know why, but he is so down.
（不知為什麼，他好沮喪。）

▶ **these days:** 近來。我建議華人講美語少用課本學的 recently。發音難又少人用。these days 是正確又不會忘記的最好美語。

例 What have you been doing these days?
（你最近都在忙些什麼？）

▶ **ought to:** 應該。美國口語用 ought to 很多。華人因為 should 只
有一個音，發音容易，同時也是「應該」的意思，所以都喜歡用
should。其實 should 含有義務性的意思，ought to 才是單純的應該，
商場上，與人共進午餐之後，這樣講是很普通的。

例 I enjoy having lunch with you. We ought to do this
more often.
(我很喜歡與您共進午餐，我們應該經常這樣做。)

HOLD SOMETHING AGAINST SOMEONE

（心懷不滿）

說明

在外做事有時難免冒犯別人。不管有意或無意，總有人因此而心懷不滿。這樣常見的事，常用的說法，怎麼可以不會呢？美國人也不例外，這句心懷不滿的話，他們也是常講的。他們說 hold 事 against 人。

【情況會話 1】 ********************

(Julie 選 John 做班長。)

Julie: I know you don't like me very much, but I do not hold it against you. I still voted for you.

（我知道你不太喜歡我，但我並不因而不滿，我還是投你一票。）

John: Thank you very much.
　　　　　（謝謝妳。）

　　　hold 是握著的意思，against 是抵制的意思。hold 事 against 人當然就是緊握一件事來抵制一個人，對他不滿。

【相關語彙】

▸ **vote for:** 投贊成票

　例 Who do you vote for, pro-life or pro-choice?
　　（你選那一方？反對人工墮胎，還是贊成人工墮胎？）

【情況會話 **2**】　*******************

(公司會議之後)

Julie: Did you see what happened in the meeting? Frank almost objected to everything David had to say.
　　　　　（你看見會議上的情形沒有？法蘭克幾乎反對大衛所說的每一句話。）

John: Yes, I saw it. I've got a feeling Frank is holding something against David. I just don't know what.
（是啊，我看到了。我有種感覺，好像法蘭克對大衛有所不滿。我只是不知道為什麼。）

▶ **object to:** 反對

囫 I don't see why we should object to having a drink together.
（我看不出為什麼要反對大家在一起喝喝酒。）

▶ **have to say:** 某某人所說的話。這句話是美國人每天都會用到的，但中國學生通常學 have to 為「必須」的意思，在這種情形下容易造成誤解。

囫 Be quiet. Let's hear what the chairman has to say.
（安靜一點！我們來聽聽主席要說什麼。）

【情況會話 3】 ***************************

(John 在抱怨。)

John: The police are too much. Every time I speed, they give me a ticket.
（警察太過分了。每次超速，他們都給我開罰單。）

Julie: There is nothing to hold against the police. You should have followed the rules.

（沒什麼好對警察不滿的，你本來就應該守規則。）

【相關語彙】

▶ **too much:** 太過分了。講什麼人 too much 不是太多，而是太過分。

例 Stop pushing her. You guys are too much.
（不要再逼她了。你們這些傢伙太過分了。）

▶ **speed:** 超速。當名詞是速度。

例 Speeding is a bad driving habit.
（超速是一種不好的駕駛習慣。）

▶ **ticket:** 罰單。本字有票券、帳單等意思。在交通法規上叫違規罰單。

例 I have never got a ticket in my twenty years of driving.
（我開了 20 年的車，還沒拿過一張罰單。）

UNIT 11

MP3-12

BACK TO BACK
(蟬聯；連續兩次)

說明

經常要說衛冕成功或蟬聯的話，但不知道該如何表達，很多華人就說成 second win，美國人聽了猛點頭，也不會糾正你，原來他們以為你要說的是第二次贏球。其實你只是不知道美語這麼簡單，用 back to back 罷了。

【情況會話 1】 *********************

(在支持的球隊連贏兩場之後。)

John: Our team is great. I love the players.
（我們的球隊很強，我喜歡他們。）

Julie: Sure the players are great. It's not easy to win back to back.
（球員真的很棒。要連贏兩場不容易啊。）

back 是背部的意思。back to back 是背靠背，一個接一個的意思，所以用在勝負的說法上，就有蟬聯、衛冕的意思。像一九九四年，美國紐約水牛美式足球隊連續四年打進冠軍賽超級杯，卻又輸了，隔天報紙上用橫幅頭條寫了一個 BACK-TO-BACK-TO-BACK-TO-BACK LOSS.

【相關語彙】

▶ **It's not easy to:** 要做什麼事不容易

例 It's not easy to bring up eight kids.
（把八個孩子養大不容易啊。）

例 It's not easy to feed 1 billion mouths in China.
（大陸能讓十億人吃飽，不容易啊。）

【情況會話 2】 *****************

（球迷之間的討論。）

Julie: Do you think our team will win today's game? That will make back-to-back wins for them.
（你看我們隊伍會贏得今天的比賽嗎？贏的話他們就連勝兩場了。）

John: Certainly they'll win.
（他們當然會贏。）

【相關語彙】

▶ **Do you think:** 你看如何？問別人對某件事的意見或看法時用的話。

例 Do you think Clinton has got a chance to win the election?
（你看克林頓有機會贏得大選嗎？）

▶ **certainly:** 當然、肯定。本字與前頁的 sure 都是表示必然有信心的意思。

例 A: May I sit with you?
（我可以坐在你旁邊嗎？）

B: Certainly.
（當然了。）

PART II

UNIT 12

BACK OUT OF SOMETHING.

（不認賬；食言毀約。）

說明

　　學校與真實社會好像有段距離，要不然現實社會中天天見得到的食言背信、不認賬的事，學校裡怎麼都沒教過英語怎麼說呢？也許是這句英語太簡單了，課本和老師都假設你已經會了。你看了這句話的說法，是否也同意，你早該會說了呢？

【情況會話 1】 *********************

(茱莉決定不去倫敦了。)

Julie: I am sorry to tell you this, but we have to postpone our trip to London.
（很抱歉告訴你，我們去倫敦玩的事要延一下。）

John: Wait a minute, Julie. We've been planning on this trip for so long, don't back out of it.
（慢著，茱莉。我們為這趟旅行計劃好久了，不要取消嘛。）

　　back 為動詞有退卻的意思，out of something 是由某件事或地點脫身。兩部分加接起來，指的是由某件事早已說定的事抽身而退，所以也是不認賬的意思。

【相關語彙】

▶ **I am sorry to:** 很遺憾地；很抱歉；這句話用得很多，大部分是外交式的開頭語，不是真正的道歉。

　例 A: David's father passed away last night.
　　　（大衛的爸爸昨晚過世了。）

　　B: I am sorry to hear it.
　　　（我感到好遺憾！）

▶ **for so long:** 好久了。用這個片語的時候，時態要用完成或完成進行式。

　例 The police have been working on the case for so long.
　　（警方辦這案子已經很久了。）

▶ **So long:** 與上句不同，So long 單獨用是再會的意思，表示分別，期待再見。

　例 So long, my friend. Hope to see you soon.
　　（再會了，朋友。希望很快會再見面。）

【情況會話 2】 ********************

(賣方跟顧客爭執。)

Seller: We had a deal. You can't back out of it now.
（我們談定的買賣，你不能不認賬。）

Buyer: I am not backing out of it. I am just asking you to make the price more reasonable.
（我可不是不認賬。我只是請您價錢上更合理一點。）

【相關語彙】

▶ **have a deal:** 談妥買賣，一言為定。

　例 After several meetings, both sides agree to have a deal.
　　（在開過幾次會議之後，雙方同意一言為定。）

▸ **asking someone to:** 要求某人做某事。

例 The new manager asked everyone to come on time.
（新的經理要求大家一定要準時到。）

【情況會話 3 】 ************************

（商業顧問對美國客戶說。）

B.C.: Remember this, it's not easy to get Chinese businessmen to agree on terms.
But, once they say yes, they mean YES.
Chinese people do not back out easily.
（記住這話，要讓中國生意人同意條件不容易。
可是，一旦他們同意，他們真的是同意。華人不輕易食言。）

【 相關語彙 】

▸ **Remember this:** 記住這句話。表示說話的權威性很強，或訓人的時候用最好。

例 Remember this, girls should not hang out too late.
（記住，女孩子不要在外面游蕩到太晚。）

▶ **agree on terms:** 同意條件

例 The Americans tried very hard to make the Japanese agree on terms, but failed.
（美方努力地要使日本同意條件，但徒勞無功。）

▶ **mean:** 當動詞有認真、不是開玩笑的意思。

例 I told you I am not going to quit. I mean it.
（我告訴過你我不會放棄。我可不是說著玩的。）

UNIT 13

AT WILL
（愛怎樣就怎樣；任意的）

說明

　　只要是我喜歡，有什麼不可以？這樣豪爽的態度，充分顯示出年輕人的活力。然而，說到用英語來表達這種大無畏的精神，恐怕很多人要垂頭喪氣吧？不用怕，學會 at will 就可以愛怎樣就怎樣。

【情況會話 1】

(自由的真意是？)

John: A lot of people misunderstand the meaning of freedom.
（許多人誤解了自由的真意。）

Julie: Yes, freedom doesn't mean a person can do anything at will. People have to care about others.
（是的，自由不意味人可以任意而為，人們也需要考慮到別人。）

【相關語彙】

▶ **care about others:** 在乎別人。care 有很多意思，基本上離不開關心和照顧的意思，這裡是指要關心別人的反應。

例 Please don't smoke in the room. You need to care about others.
（請不要在室內抽煙，你得為別人想一想。）

【情況會話 2】 ＊＊＊＊＊＊＊＊＊＊＊＊＊＊＊＊＊＊＊＊＊

(Julie 的門鈴響，她開了門。)

Julie: Hi, John. Come on in. Make yourself at home.
（嗨，約翰！進來吧，不要客氣。）

John: I like to come over. You are so nice. I can eat anything at will in your house.
（我最愛到妳家。你人真好，在妳這兒我愛吃什麼就吃什麼。）

【相關語彙】

▶ **come on in:** 表示很熱情地邀請進門。比 come in 語氣
強。

　例 Come on in. We have been waiting for you.
　　（進來吧，我們一直在等你。）

▶ **make yourself at home:** 不要客氣，要什麼就自己
動手，別拘泥的意思。特別用在拿東西請客人的時候。

　例 Try a piece of cake. Make yourself at
　　home.
　　（吃塊蛋糕吧。別客氣。）

▶ **come over:** 到別人家或自己家裡來。

　例 I would like to invite you to come over this
　　Sunday.
　　（我想邀請你這個星期天到我家來。）

【情況會話 **3**】 ************************

(John 有個「封建」家庭。)

John:　We have a lot of rules at home. We have to
　　　　follow all of them except for my father. He
　　　　does all kinds of things at will.

（我們家裡規矩好多。除了我老爸以外，我們都得遵守。他可以愛做什麼就做什麼。）

Julie: And, he must be the one who made all the rules for you. Right?
（那，他一定就是訂下這些規矩的人了，是不是？）

【相關語彙】

▶ **except for:** 除了某人或某事之外。

例 Everyone showed up at the meeting except for John.
（除了 John 以外，人人都出席了會議。）

▶ **must be:** 一定是。這個用語是表示推測，不是表示肯定。

例 Your girlfriend must be very pretty.
（你的女朋友一定很漂亮。）

例 I see a lot of people running on the street. There must be something wrong.
（我看見許多人在街上跑。一定有什麼事不對勁。）

THE LAST THING
（最不喜歡的事）

說明

　　這個 the last 的用法，不只可以加 thing，表示最不喜歡的事，也可以加任何名詞，表示最不喜歡的人、事或其他東西。英語教授對這個詞有偏好，大學聯考試題就出過幾回，托福考試更不用說。

【情況會話 1】 ＊＊＊＊＊＊＊＊＊＊＊＊＊＊＊＊＊＊＊＊＊＊＊

(中美貿易談判。)

John: What do you think about the trade talk between Taiwan and the U.S.?
（對台灣和美國的貿易談判，妳的看法如何？）

Julie: Well, I expect some type of compromise. The last thing both sides want is a trade war.
（我預期會有某種型式的折衷方案。雙方最不喜歡的事就是貿易戰爭。）

老式電影中，女主角對男主角撒嬌說：「就算世上男人只剩你一個，我也不嫁給你。」就是這個意思了。The last 指最後，在此表示最不可能、最不喜歡、最不願意。

【相關語彙】

▶ **trade talk:** 貿易談判。

例 Japan and the United States broke off in their trade talks.
（日本和美國的貿易談判破裂。）

▶ **well:** 用在句子起頭，是一種沈吟思考的聲音，沒有特別意思。但用得特別多。

例 Well, can I leave now?
（好了，我可以離開了嗎？）

【情況會話 2】 ********************

(John 在大嘆倒楣。)

John: Lightning really strikes twice in the same spot. The last thing I wanted my mother to know was I had failed in the exam, but the

report card went directly to her.
(屋漏偏逢連夜雨。我最不喜歡我媽知道的事就是我考不及格，偏偏成績單讓她收到了。)

Julie: Don't you think your Mom has the right to know how you are doing in school?
(你難道不認為令堂有權利知道你在學校的表現？)

【相關語彙】

▸ **Lightning really strikes twice on the same spot.:** 閃電真的兩次擊中同一點。華人說「屋漏偏逢連夜雨」。

▸ **fail in the exam:** 考試不及格。美語中不喜歡用 examination 而簡單用 exam。

例 For those who failed in the exam, there will be a make up test.
(針對考不及格的人，有一個補考機會。)

▸ **have the right to know:** 有權利知道。

例 In addition to freedom, the people want to have the right to know.
(除了自由以外，人民更要有知的權利。)

AT SEA

（茫然不懂，摸不著頭緒）

說明

　　本句指腦中一片茫然，完全不清楚怎麼一回事。就如同在海上，到處一望無際，不知身在何處，何去何從。特別用在工作場合或學校功課為多。

【情況會話 1】 **************************

(John 正在為數學傷腦筋。)

John: I've really got a problem with my math. I am totally at sea about it.
（我的數學問題很大，我完全不懂。）

Julie: Don't worry. I will be happy to help you out.
（別擔心，我很樂意幫你忙。）

茫然摸不清頭緒就如同在海上一般，這樣就永遠不會忘記了。本句另一個說法叫 out of sea，出到海洋上，一樣是指對事情毫不清楚。要是特別說明不清楚某件事，則在後面加 about。

【相關語彙】

▶ **have got a problem with:** 對某事或某人有困難或矛盾。

例 The Lions lost their game again. I think they have got a problem with batting.
（獅隊又輸球了。我想他們的打擊有問題。）

▶ **help someone out:** 幫忙某人脫離困境，比單用 help someone 更有解決問題的涵意。

例 We need more people to help us out on the project so we can finish it on time.
（我們需要更多人幫忙做這個專案，好準時完成它。）

【情況會話 2】 ***********************

(在辦公室裡。)

John: Maybe you can help me on this. What does Mr. Lee really want?
(妳也許可以幫幫我，到底李先生要什麼？)

Julie: Oh, poor Johnny. You seem totally at sea.
(噢！可憐的 Johnny，你好像一點頭緒都沒有。)

【相關語彙】

▸ **Maybe you can help me:** 請別人幫忙不一定要用 Would you please 這種求人的語氣，特別是熟人之間，儘管用本句。

▸ **Oh, poor Johnny.:** 說話的時候，故意表示同情別人。注意聽錄意帶中的語調，這種語調在美語中，對熟人說話時常用。另外，記得在對方名字的尾音加上 [ɪ] 的音，如 Frank 變成 Franky。

【情況會話 3】 ***********************

(抱怨台北的交通。)

John: What happened to the officials in Taipei? Don't they realize how bad the traffic is.

The whole city is a parking lot.
（台北市的官員怎麼啦？他們難道不知道交通有
多糟？全市成了一個停車場。）

Julie: They know the problem. They are just at
sea about the solution.
（他們知道問題，只是不知道用什麼方法來解
決。）

【相關語彙】

▶ **What happened to someone:** 某人怎麼了

    例 What happened to you? You are all wet.
    （你怎麼了，渾身都溼透了。）

▶ **official:** 政府官員

▶ **realize:** 理解

    例 Kids don't realize how much parents love
    them.
    （孩子們不知道父母多愛他們。）

▶ **a parking lot:** 停車場。美語喜歡用它來形容交通阻塞。

    例 Because of the accident, the highway
    became a parking lot.
    （因為發生車禍，整條高速公路成停車場。）

UNIT 16

AT LARGE

（消遙法外；尚未逮著）

說明

本句不僅用在尚未捕獲的犯人，只要是任何東西，還在海闊天空，還沒回到應該在的地方，都可以用 at large 來說明。

【情況會話 1】 **********************

(約翰和茱莉在談論走失的小鳥。)

Julie: My parrot flew away the other day. He is still at large.
（我的鸚鵡前幾天飛走了，還沒有回來。）

John: Think of the bright side. He is free now.
（往好的方面想吧！牠現在自由了。）

large 是大而寬闊的意思。at large 指天地廣闊，任其逍遙，於是借來形容尚未就逮的事物。另外 at large 如放在名詞團體之後，動詞之前，可以表示該團體的大部分成員。請看相關語彙中的例子。

【相關語彙】

▶ **the other day:** 前幾天

例 We saw David the other day.
（我們前幾天看見大衛。）

▶ **Think of the bright side:** 往好的方面想。這句美語用在安慰別人；告訴別人塞翁失馬焉知非福的時候，起頭先說這一句，一定沒錯。

例 Frank lost his job. But think of the bright side, he can do whatever he wants to do, now.
（法蘭克丟了他的工作，可是往好的方面想，他現在可以做他想做的事了。）

▶ **(some group) at large:** 大部分成員

例 The students at large thought Mr. Lee was the best teacher.
（大部分的學生都認為李老師是最好的老師。）

【情況會話 2】 *********************

(兩人正在談論社會新聞。)

John: The police have to work harder to solve the murder case before the killer kills again.
(警方在凶手再次殺人之前，要多加把勁把這個凶殺案破了才行。)

Julie: Yes, I am sure the police won't let the murderer be at large too long. They'll corner him.
(是啊，我想警方不會讓凶手逍遙法外太久，他們會逮到他的。)

【相關語彙】

▸ **murder case:** 凶殺案。華人經常誤解 murder 的意思，以為是有計劃性的謀殺。事實上，只要是凶殺案都可以用 murder。

　例 It seems more than one person involving in the murder case.
(似乎不只一人涉及這個凶殺案。)

▸ **corner someone:** 逮到某人

　例 I'll corner whoever stole my purse.
(我會逮著偷我錢包的人。)

ASK SOMEONE OUT
（請某人出去約會）

> **說明**
>
> 　　見到自己心儀的小姐，想約出去談心，不會說這樣的英語太遜了吧？尤其是像 ask out 這麼簡單的英語。華人對這句話可別誤解成要找某人出去單挑打架噢！

【情況會話 1】 **********************

(約翰想和瑪莉約會。)

John:　I like Mary. I wish I can know more about her.
（我喜歡瑪莉，真希望能多瞭解她。）

Julie:　It's easy. All you have to do is, ask her out.
（那容易，邀她出去約會就得了。）

還記得 ask 有要求的意思嗎？ ask out 就是邀約出去的意思。美語用法只用在男女約會，這方面別按字面誤用。

【相關語彙】

▶ **know more about:** 更瞭解一點

　例 I would like to know more about the product.
（我想對這個產品更瞭解一些。）

▶ **it's easy:** 那容易。指容易辦到。

　例 I can reach the top in three seconds. It's easy.
（我可以在三秒之內到達頂端。這太容易了。）

▶ **it's simple:** 那容易。指事情不複雜。

　例 A:　How do you know he is not coming?
（你怎麼曉得他不來？）

　　 B:　It's simple.I did not invite him.
（簡單得很。我根本沒邀他。）

▸ **All you have to do is:** 僅僅這樣做就得了。

例 Rice cooking is easy. All you have to do is buy a rice cooker.
（煮飯很容易。買個電鍋就成了。）

【情況會話 2】 **********************

（約翰被瑪莉拒於門外）

| John: | Is there any way to ask Mary out? I have been trying very hard, but she turned me down every time.
（有沒有辦法約瑪莉出去呢？我一直努力去嘗試，但她每回都拒絕了。） |

| Julie: | Keep trying. One of these days, you may be in luck.
（繼續試。總有一天，你會走運的。） |

【相關語彙】

▸ **Is there any way to....?:** 有沒有辦法

例 Is there any way to get rich overnight?
（有沒有辦法一夜致富？）

▶ **turn someone down:** 拒絕人家的提議

例 I invited Julie to lunch, but she turned me down.
（我邀茉莉去吃午餐，但她拒絕了。）

▶ **keep:** 加動名詞，表示一直在做的意思。

例 Keep thinking. You may find out the answer.
（再想想看。你也許會發現答案。）

▶ **one of these days:** 總有那麼一天

例 Well, one of these days, you'll see I am a good guy.
（唉！總有一天你會明白我是好人。）

【情況會話 3】 ***********************

（當面邀約）

John: Is there any possibility in this world that I may ask you out?
（我到底有沒有可能約妳出來？）

Julie: Not until the sun rises in the west.
（除非太陽從西邊出來。）

【相關語彙】

▶ **in the world:** 在這個世界上。用做加強語氣表示究竟、到底的意思，the 也可以用 this。

　例 What in the world are you doing?
　　（你到底在幹嘛？）

▶ **not until:** 直到（某種情況、時間）之前都不會。

　例 I don't believe your story. Not until you prove it.
　　（在你證明事實之前，我不會相信你說的故事。）

▶ **not a chance:** 毫不可能。本節對話，茱莉的回答也可以用本句。

　例 A: Can you loan me some money?
　　　（借點錢給我可以嗎？）

　　 B: Not a chance.
　　　（門都沒有。）

UNIT 18

ALL TOLD

（總的來說；整個來看）

說明

　　說話中，有時要做個總結。在說了一大堆理由或情況之後，來一句 all told，會使你的英語聽眾覺得你的英語很溜。

【情況會話 1】 ********************

（談政治。）

Julie: What do you think of our president?
（你覺得我們總統如何？）

John: Well, all told, he is a good one. I like him.
（這個嘛，總而言之，他幹得很好。我喜歡他。）

英語表示就這樣了或結束，叫 That's all。當我們說一個人或一件事，可能牽涉到幾個重點，最後要來個總結，當然是用 All told，都說完了，可以總結了。

【相關語彙】

▶ **net ane net:** All told 的另一個常見說法。

例 He may have a lot of shortcomings, but net and net, he is a good guy.
(他也許有許多缺點，但整體來說，他還算是個好人。)

【情況會話 **2**】 *************************

(談經濟)

Julie: Do you really think the economy is going to be better next year?
(你真的認為明年經濟情況會好一點？)

John: A lot of things may happen between now and next year. But, all told, I would think so.
(現在到明年之間有很多事可能發生，不過，總而言之，我想是吧。)

▶ **economy:** 經濟

  例 China is focusing on improving its economy.
  (大陸致力於改善經濟。)

▶ **economic:** 雖是 economy 的形容詞，卻是節約、經濟型的意思。

  例 I can only afford economic class.
  (我只負擔得起經濟艙。)

▶ **I would think so.:** I think so. 是很明確表示我這樣想。加一個 would 就是我想大概是如此吧。語氣比較不肯定。

  例 A: do you think Frank can do a good job on this?
  (你認為法蘭克可以把這個工作做好嗎？)

  B: I would think so.
  (大概會吧！)

【情況會話 3】 ********************

(談論朋友。)

John: A simple job like what Frank is doing won't make much money.
(法蘭克做的工作那樣簡單，賺不了什麼錢的。)

Julie: Yes, a simple job like that won't make much. But he has a lot of customers. So, all told, he still has a very good income.
(是的。像那麼簡單的工作是賺不了幾個錢。但他客人多,所以總體來說,他收入還是很好。)

【 相關語彙 】

▶ **simple:** 不複雜。看下面的例句,華人不太會分 simple 和 easy。

例 It's a simple job, but if you don't know the right way to do it, it's still not easy.
(工作並不複雜,但若不知正確的做法,還是不容易做。)

▶ **make money:** 掙錢

例 My dream is to make a lot of money.
(我的夢想是賺大錢。)

▶ **good income:** 高收入

例 Education is the key to good income.
(教育程度是高收入的關鍵。)

UNIT 19

ALL THUMBS
（一竅不通；笨手笨腳）

說明

當我們談到某件事情，要表明實在不會做，最簡單的說法就是 All thumbs. 當某人做起某事來笨手笨腳的，也可以用 All thumbs 來形容。

【情況會話 1 】 *********************

(做事笨手笨腳。)

Julie: When it comes to gardening, I am all thumbs.
（說到蒔花種菜，我是一竅不通。）

John: I am not good at gardening, either.
（我也不太行。）

　　thumb 是大姆指,一個人手巧才有辦法把工作做好,若是 10 根指頭都成了大姆指,還指望手巧嗎?當然是笨手笨腳的了。

【相關語彙】

▶ **When it comes to....:** 說到,提起

　例 when it comes to math, no one in my class can beat John.
　(提起數學,我們班上沒人勝得過約翰。)

▶ **good at:** 在行;很懂

　例 Let John do it. He is good at it.
　(讓約翰來做,他行得很。)

【情況會話 2】 ***********************

(一竅不通。)

John: Can you help me with this math problem?
(你能幫我解這道數學題嗎?)

Julie: Oh, no. Please leave me alone. You know I am all thumbs with math.
(噢不!別煩我。你知道我對數學一竅不通。)

▶ **help someone with:** 幫人做某件事

例 My sister is helping my Mom with dishes.
（我姐姐幫我老媽洗碗。）

▶ **math problem:** 數學題目。這裡的 problem 不是困難
之意。

例 Chinese students are good at solving math
problems.
（中國學生對數學方面有一套。）

▶ **leave me alone:** 別煩我。

例 Would you please leave me alone?
（請別煩我好不好？）

【情況會話 3】 ********************

(技術欠佳。)

John: Frank can't play the piano at all. He is all
thumbs.
（法蘭克根本不會彈鋼琴。他笨手笨腳的。）

Julie: Sure he can't. It sounds real bad.
（他當然不會，聲音聽起來糟透了。）

【相關語彙】

▶ **play the piano:** 彈鋼琴

例 It takes years to learn how to play the
piano.
（學鋼琴要花好多年。）

▶ **sound:** 當動詞是聽起來如何的意思，後面要加形容詞或
名詞做補語。

例 A: How about having a drink?
（來杯酒如何？）

B: It sounds a good idea.
（聽起來是個好主意。）

UNIT 20

AFTER HOURS
（打烊之後）

說明

> 很多活動都在打烊後才開始的。所以邀約辦事常常要用到 after hours。請注意 after hours 和 after work 不同，後者是下班的意思。

【情況會話 1】 ********************

(商店打烊之後。)

John: We need to get everybody together for some drinks.
（我們得把大家找齊再一起喝酒。）

Julie: You can't do that during work. Maybe we can do it after hours.
（上班時間不可以這樣做。等打烊之後再說吧！）

　　　hours 是一段時間，做某一種特殊用途，如 lunch hour 是午餐時間。在這裡指營業時間。after hours 就是營業結束，大家散工之後。

【相關語彙】

▶ **get everybody together:** 把大家找齊。

　🖾 Let's get everybody together to have a meeting.
　（讓我們把大家找齊來開會。）

▶ **during work:** 上班時

　🖾 Drinking is not allowed during work.
　（上班時不許喝酒。）

【情況會話 2】 ********************

(打烊之後的狀況。)

John:　There is one thing I noticed so different from Taiwan when I was in America.
（我在美國時，發現一件與台灣很不同的事。）

Julie:　What was that?
（是什麼？）

John: Stores never turn the lights off after hours.
（商店打烊後不關燈。）

【相關語彙】

▸ **noticed:** 注意到

例 I noticed Julie was not happy.
（我注意到茱莉不太高興。）

▸ **What was that?** 別人說話沒說清楚，或沒聽清楚時，用本句再問他一次。

例 A: My father set a new rule for us.
（我老爸給我們訂了一條新規則。）

B: What was that?
（是什麼？）

A: No talking during the meal.
（吃飯時不許說話。）

【情況會話 3】 *********************

（下班後。）

John: Can I see you sometime?
（我能不能去找妳？）

Julie:　Yes, we can go somewhere. Or if you prefer, you can come to my office after hours, there will be no one else but just us.
（行。我們可以找個地方。或是你喜歡的話，可以在我公司打烊之後來我辦公室。除了我們之外不會有別人。）

【相關語彙】

▶ **Can I see you sometime?:** 男女之間約會的用語。

▶ **if you prefer:** 你比較喜歡的話。

例 You can take a bus. But if you prefer, taxies are also available.
（你可以坐公車，但如果你比較喜歡坐計程車也可以。）

▶ **no one else but us:** 除了我們，別無他人。這裡的 but 是除了的意思。

例 No one else knows the truth but us.
（除了我們，沒人知道真象。）

UNIT 21

BUG SOMEONE
（麻煩、打擾別人）

說明

　　bug 原意是臭蟲，美語用這個字的情形很多。本句是指去麻煩或打擾別人。要麻煩別人的時候，可以用第二情況會話的例子做起頭。通常被麻煩的人一聽你這麼客氣，大概都不會拒絕你的要求。

【情況會話 1】 **********************

(老公對老婆。)

Husband: Take the kid away. He's been bugging me all morning.
（把小孩帶開。他已經吵了我一早上了。）

Wife: All right. He's just trying to play with you. That's all.
（好啦。他只不過想和你玩嘛。如此而已。）

　　　bug 是小蟲。美語中喜歡用來指細小卻不好容忍的東西，如流行性感冒叫 flu bug。bug 用作動詞，指吵得人家難以專心做事。

【相關語彙】

▶ **take someone away:** 把人帶開

　例 I can't stand the kid's noise. Take him away.
　（我受不了小孩吵。把他帶開。）

▶ **That's all.:** 如此而已。

　例 I come to say goodbye. That's all.
　（我只是來告別，如此而已。）

【情況會話 2】 ***********************

(約翰又問茱莉同一個題目。)

John:　Sorry to bug you again. But I still don't know how to solve the problem. Can you show me again?
　　　（對不起又來麻煩你，可我還是不會這道題，妳能再做一次讓我看嗎？）

Julie: O.K. But you've got to pay attention this time.
（可以。但這回你要仔細看了。）

【相關語彙】

▶ **Sorry to bug you.:** 對不起來麻煩你。當別人在做他自己的事，而你必須請他幫忙，記得用這句話。

例 Sorry to bug you. Would you please tell me where the file is?
（對不起麻煩你。請告訴我檔案在那裡？）

▶ **Can you show me:** show 不一定是展示。這句話是請人做或指給你看。

例 Can you show me how to get to the station?
（你能告訴我怎樣可以到車站嗎？）

【情況會話 3】 ********************

（*男生對女生。*）

Julie: The teacher gave Frank a very serious warning today.
（今天老師給法蘭克一個嚴重的警告。）

John: What's wrong with him?
（他怎麼了？）

Julie: He kept bugging the girls in class.
（他上課老愛作弄女生。）

【相關語彙】

▶ **serious warning:** 嚴重警告

例 Let me give you a serious warning. Don't ever drink again during work.
（我鄭重警告你，上班時間絕對不可再喝酒。）

▶ **pay attention:** 注意

例 I am going to assign the work. I want you all to pay attention.
（我要開始分派工作。你們大家注意聽。）

UNIT 22

BY THE SAME TOKEN

（同樣地，一體兩面）

說明

　　跟外國人用英語交談，最怕不會辯論道理，遇到事情被人家一頓搶白就目瞪口呆。趕快把這句話記起來。有人對你說你應該如何如何，就頂他一句，by the same token, you too. 同樣地，你自己該如何如何。

【情況會話 1】 ***********************

(討論人與人間的關係。)

John: I don't like people to bug me. By the same token, I try not to bug others.
（我不喜歡人家吵我，同樣地，我儘量不吵別人。）

Julie: You sound like a very reasonable man.
（聽起來，你是個很講理的人囉！）

by 的意思很多，這裡指使用。token 是銅板、小零錢，做投幣用的，有正反兩面。By the same token 是如同錢幣的正反兩面，都一樣的意思。

【相關語彙】

▶ **try not to:** 試著不要，儘量不要。not 加在 try to 中間。

例 I tried not to wake up the baby.
（我盡量不吵醒小嬰兒。）

▶ **reasonable:** 講東西是指合理，講人是指頭腦清楚可以講道理。

例 The price is reasonable.
（價錢還算合理。）

例 Any reasonable man would decide what John had done was wrong.
（任何有理性的人都會判斷約翰的作為是錯的。）

【情況會話2】 ******************

（談兩岸關係。）

Julie:　What do you think can make peace between China and Taiwan?
（你認為台灣和大陸怎樣才能達成和平？）

John: Well, First I think China has to do something to show their good will. And by the same token, Taiwan can help China to build a strong economy.
（首先，我認為大陸須要表示善意。同樣的，台灣也可以幫大陸建設強大的經濟。）

【相關語彙】

▶ **make peace between:** 兩方達成和平。

例 The United States tried very hard to make peace between Isreal and the Arabs.
（美國努力地要讓以色列和阿拉伯國家達成和平。）

▶ **good will:** 善意

例 Chinese people like to give for good will and not take for return.
（華人喜歡善意給予而不求回報。）

▶ **build a strong economy:** 建立強大的經濟。

例 The first thing that China has to do is build a strong economy.
（大陸第一要務是建立強大的經濟。）

UNIT 23

MP3-24

CALL IT A DAY

（今天到此為止。）

說明

　　這句話用在任何場合都行，上班、學校、家庭等都可以使用。只要是不再做了，要結束了，就可以用。假如是在晚上，則可以把 day 改成 night，意思一樣。

【情況會話 1】　************************

John:　It's late. Let's call it a day.
（不早了。今天到此為止吧。）

Julie:　No,let's finish the job before we go.
（不，等我們做完了再走。）

記憶法

　　call 是叫或稱呼。Call it a day 是指到此就算是一天吧，所以就是不再做了。

【相關語彙】

▶ **It's late.:** 天色不早了，注意本句不是遲到的意思。

　　例 Let's go home. It's late.
　　　（回家吧！天不早了。）

▶ **It's too late.:** 太遲了。本句指於事無補。

　　例 It's too late. The hurt is done.
　　　（太遲了。傷害已經造成。）

【情況會話 2】

****

（約翰正走出辦公室。）

John: See you all tomorrow.
　　　（大家明天見。）

Julie: Are you calling it a day, so early?
　　　（你要下班了？這麼早？）

John: Yes, I'll take the rest of the day off.
　　　（不錯，我下午請假。）

【相關語彙】

▶ **See you tommorrow:** 明天見。Good bye 的意思。

▶ **the rest of the day:** 今天剩下的時間，美語通常指做到某個段落之後的整個下午時間。

> 例 I have finished all the jobs. I don't know what else to do for the rest of the day.
> （我工作都做完了，剩下的時間不曉得要幹嘛。）

▶ **take (time) off:** 請假。本句中 time 可以用任何時間單位。

> 例 I feel so tired. I need to take one day off.
> （我覺得好累，我需要請一天假。）

【情況會話 3】 *********************

Julie: It's time to go. Come on, call it a day.
（時間差不多了。走吧！今天到此為止。）

John: O.K. I am coming.
（好！我就來。）

▶ **It's time to go.:** 時間差不多，該走了。

例 Are you all ready? It's time to go.
（你們全都準備好了嗎？該走了。）

▶ **I'm coming.:** 我就來。當人家在等你，你可以用這句叫他再等一下。

例 A: Hurry up. We are going to be late.
（快點，我們要遲到了。）

B: O.K. I'm coming.
（好啦，我就來。）

PART III

UNIT 24

SOMEONE IS CANNED

（被炒魷魚了）

說明

　　這句話多用在工作場合，指某人丟了工作。華人一般都喜歡用 fired。除非你明確知道丟掉工作的人是做錯事而被開除，不然不要用 fired，用 canned。意思相近，涵蓋較廣。

【情況會話 1】 *********************

John: Frank was canned today.
（法蘭克今天被吵魷魚了。）

Julie: You mean he was fired?
（你是說他被開除？）

John: Yes.
（是的。）

can 原意是能夠。也有銅罐或裝罐子的意思。這裡用被動式,指被塞進罐子,有被逮著的意思。在工作場合再引申為被逮著而失去工作。

【相關語彙】

▶ **someone is fired:** 因為嚴重過失而被開除。

🔟 Frank was fired because he got kickback from the customers.
(法蘭克因為跟顧客拿回扣而被開除了。)

▶ **someone was laid off:** 被資遣。通常因公司賠錢或遷廠。

🔟 Frank was laid off from work because the company lost a lot of money.
(因為公司賠了很多錢,法蘭克被資遣了。)

【情況會話 2】 *******************

John: Frank just walked out of the door when he got canned.
(法蘭克一失去工作就直接走出去。)

Julie: So, he didn't even take his personal stuff with him.
（那麼，他連私人東西都沒帶走？）

John: No.
（沒有。）

【相關語彙】

▶ **walk out of the door:** 走出去、離開的意思。

例 Before we find out who stole the money, no one is to walk out of the door.
（在我們找出誰偷了錢之前，誰也不許離開。）

▶ **personal stuff:** 私人東西。

例 You can't bring your personal stuff into the classroom during the exam.
（考試的時候，不可以帶私人東西到教室裡。）

UNIT 25

MP3-26

CARRY THE BALL

(負責全局)

說明

這個字最叫華人誤解,因為照字面翻譯它叫「帶球跑」。特別是這個字用在女士身上的時候,華人一定自以為懂,卻是相差十萬八千里。學英語,要小心啊!

【情況會話 1】 *********************

John: After Frank leaves, who will carry the ball in your office?
(法蘭克離開之後,你們辦公室將由誰來領導?)

Julie: We are not sure yet. I hope they will promote someone from inside the office.
(我們還不知道。我希望他們會從辦公室內部挑一個人升上來。)

美國人嗜球賽成性，他們用球賽比喻人生，就好像華人用戲劇比喻人生一樣普遍。carry the ball 是帶球跑的人，球到那裡，大家自然跟到那裡，所以引申為領導的意思。

【相關語彙】

▶ **promote:** 升遷

例 Mr. Lee was promoted to be in charge of the business in China and Taiwan.
（李先生調升來領導大陸和台灣二地的商務。）

▶ **in charge:** 與 carry the ball 的意思一樣，但言語上比較普通，不生動。

例 Who is in charge in your office?
（你們辦公室是誰在負責？）

【情況會話 2】 **************************

John: In Chinese tradition, whoever carries the ball has the last words.
（中國傳統，官大學問大。）

Julie: Same thing in America. You can't argue
with your boss too much.
(在美國也一樣，你跟上司不能太計較。)

【相關語彙】

▶ **the last words:** 最後發言權。指權威性的裁奪。

例 At home, my father has the last words.
(在家裡，我爸爸有絕對權威決定事情。)

▶ **same thing here:** 我也一樣。本句中 here 可以用任何
地點來取代，表示當地也一樣。

例 A: I lost a lot of money in the stock.
(我投資股票賠了好多錢。)

B: Same thing here. It ate up all my
savings.
(我也一樣。我的儲蓄全給吃掉了。)

▶ **argue with:** 與人爭論或計較。

例 I am not going to argue with you.
(我不跟你爭辯。)

UNIT 26

CASH IN ON
（靠著賺大錢；大撈一筆。）

說明

　　講到賺錢，許多人以為英語就只有 make money 或 get rich 的說法而已。其實，英語是很漂亮的語言，跟中國話一樣，生動活潑，多采多姿。大部分人學法錯誤，把它想得太難了。像 cash in on 三個單字都那麼簡單，合在一起就有著著實實地收上一筆錢的意思。

【情況會話 1】　******************

（在冬季奧運之後。）

John: Nancy was very happy to win a gold medal in the Winter Olympics.
（南茜很高興在冬季奧運贏得金牌。）

Julie: Yes, now she can cash in on it.
（是啊！這下她可以大撈一筆了。）

cash 是現金，cash in 是收進一筆現金，on 有依靠的意思。所以合起來是大撈一筆。

【相關語彙】

▶ **gold medal:** 金牌、冠軍

囫 China won three gold medals in swimming.
（大陸在游泳項目贏得三面金牌。）

▶ **Winter Olympics:** 冬季奧運

▶ **Summer Olympics:** 夏季奧運

【情況會話 2】 **********************

John: After several years of testing. Ford finally got the new car out in the market.
（在多年的測試之後，福特公司終於把新款車推出市場銷售。）

Julie: Yes, the company was very careful about the new car. They hope to cash in on it big this time.
（是的，福特公司對這部車很小心，他們希望這回可以狠狠地熱賣一番。）

▶ **get something out in the market:** 推出銷售。

例 When do you expect the company to get the new product out in the market?
（你預計公司幾時會把新產品推出銷售？）

▶ **big:** 狠狠地，大大地。

例 A:　do you play the lottery?
　　　（你玩彩券嗎？）

　　B:　Yes, I want to win big.
　　　（玩。我要大大地贏一筆。）

UNIT 27

REAL GOOD
（徹徹底底的；很詳盡的）

說明

　　英語單字記得多的人，可能可以說 thorough 這個字叫徹底。問題是大部份人連發音都有困難。不信查查字典，看它的不同發音，再按著音標唸唸看。其實，說話的時候，講徹底，沒有一個字眼好過 real good 了。又好記，又好講，說出來又容易懂，何樂而不為呢？

【情況會話 1】 *********************

John: Sorry to bug you again, but I still don't understand this problem.
（對不起，又打擾妳了。我還是不明白這道題。）

Julie: All right, I'll show you one more time.
This time I want you to watch me real
good when I am solving it.

（好。我再做給你看一次。這回我解題的時候，
我要你徹徹底底地看清楚。）

　　real 是真的，good 是很好。兩個字擺在一塊，是
真正地、好好地的意思，也就是徹徹底底的。有時候，
看句子的意思，如果句子講的是反面的意思，也可以用
real bad 來取代 real good。

【相關語彙】

▶ **one more time:** 再一次，again 的意思。

例 Let's cheer Nancy one more time for her
win in the Winter Olympics.
（讓我們再為南茜贏得冬季奧運歡呼。）

【情況會話 **2**】 ＊＊＊＊＊＊＊＊＊＊＊＊＊＊＊＊＊＊＊＊＊

John: After several years of testing. Ford finally got the new car out in the market.
(在多年測試之後，福特終於把新款車推出市場。)

Julie: Yes, they take the new car very seriously. They want to make sure they can cash in on it real good.
(是的，他們對這款新車是很認真的，他們要確知可以徹底的大賺一筆。)

【相關語彙】

▶ **take something seriously:** 很嚴肅認真地看待某件事

例 I want you to take the job seriously.
(我要你把工作看認真一點。)

▶ **make sure:** 確定

例 Before you leave the office, make sure all the doors are locked.
(離開辦公室之前，要確定所有的門都鎖上了。)

COUNT HEADS
（清點人數，點人頭）

說明

開會選擇的時候，一定要清點人數。英語的說法保證你在本書這裡一學，一輩子不會忘記，用 count heads 就可以了。

【情況會話 1 】 ＊＊＊＊＊＊＊＊＊＊＊＊＊＊＊＊＊＊＊＊＊＊＊

Julie: We didn't choose our class leader today.
（我們今天沒選班長。）

John: why not?
（為什麼？）

Julie: Well, we counted heads and there were not enough people showing up to vote.
（我們算算人數，出席選舉的人數不足。）

count 是算的意思，count heads 就是點人頭。美語中也有人用 count noses 點鼻子，聽起來有些怪，不如 count heads 用得多。

【相關語彙】

▶ **Why not:** 為什麼不。它有三種不同用法：第一是用於別人說他不要或沒做某件事，你問理由時；第二種是給別人建議；第三是別人問你要不要做某件事，你回答當然要時用。

例 A:　I don't eat much.
　　　　（我吃得不多。）

　　B:　Why not?
　　　　（為什麼？）

　　A:　I am on a diet.
　　　　（我在節食。）

例 Why not just close the business if you don't make money?
（不賺錢的話為什麼不乾脆把生意收起來算了？）

例 A:　Do you want some coffee?
　　　　（要不要喝咖啡？）

　　B:　Yes, why not?
　　　　（好啊，可以啊。）

【情況會話 2】 **********************

John: I think everybody is here. Shall we start the meeting now?
（我想大家到齊了。我們現在就開會嗎？）

Julie: No, let's count heads first, to make sure everybody is here.
（不，先算算人數，確定大家都在。）

【相關語彙】

▶ **shall we:** 我們可以這樣做了嗎？它的用法有兩種。第一是單純的詢問別人的意見；另一種是要大家一起做的事，然後禮貌性地附加一句可以嗎。這樣的用法，文法上叫附加問句。

例 Shall we invite David to come over?
（我們要邀請大衛來我們家嗎？）

例 Let's invite David to come over, shall we?
（我們來邀請大衛到我們家，可以嗎？）

UNIT 29

MP3-30

CUT CORNERS
（偷工減料，投機取巧）

說明

做買賣一定要保護自己的權益，要是對方投機取巧，偷工減料，絕不能吃悶虧。如何用英語來投訴呢？cut corners 就是你一定要會說的一句英語，簡單有效。

【情況會話 1】 ************************

Julie: I like to deal with American businessmen.
（我喜歡跟美國商人做生意。）

John: Any special reason for that?
（有特殊的理由嗎？）

Julie: Yes. Normally they don't cut corners. They give you what you expect.
（有。通常他們不會偷工減料。他們會按你預期的東西給你。）

cut 是截斷，corners 是角落。你訂了東西，他把四個角切掉，給你一個缺角的東西，當然是偷工減料了。

【相關語彙】

▶ **deal with:** 後面接人是指接觸談生意；接事是指處理。

例 I like to deal with John. He is honest.
（我喜歡與約翰談生意。他滿誠實的。）

例 This job is not too hard to do. I can deal with it.
（這件事不難做，我可以處理得來。）

【情況會話 2】 ***********************

John: I can't believe the highway is so bumpy. I think it was just built less than a year ago.
（我不敢相信這條公路顛簸得這樣厲害。我以為才建好不到一年。）

Julie: It's not unusual at all. The builders always cut corners.
（沒什麼不尋常。營造商常常偷工減料。）

【相關語彙】

▸ **less than time:** 不到多少時間。本句的 time 可以用任何時間單位取代。

例 I have known John for less than a month, but we became good friends.
（我認識約翰不到一個月，但現在我們是好朋友。）

▸ **not at all:** not 與 at 中間可以放任何形容詞或副詞，表示一點也不怎麼樣。若僅是 not at all 連用，則可以表示不謝，等於 You are welcome。

例 The work is not hard at all. I can deal with it.
（工作一點都不難。我可以處理。）

例 A: Thank you for your help.
（謝謝你的幫忙。）

B: Not at all.
（不客氣。）

UNIT 30

CUT BACK ON SOMETHING

（緊縮）

說明

　　勝敗乃兵家常事。特別是做生意或家庭開支，收入不夠，要在某些開銷上緊縮以求度過難關是正常的。所以這句話也成了經濟不景氣時，大家口頭上常用的一句話。很容易記得的。

【情況會話 1】 ********************

John: Frank got canned today.
（法蘭克今天被炒魷魚。）

Julie: Yes, the company is not making money. They have to cut back on staff.
（是啊，公司不賺錢，他們必須裁員。）

cut 是截斷，back 是縮回來，on 是在某些東西上面。三個字合起來，cut back on 指在某些東西上裁一裁、縮一縮，所以表示緊縮。

【相關語彙】

▸ **have to:** 必須。有逼不得已，不得不做的意思。若是指義務性的必須，可以用 must 來代替。

例 For the good of my country, I have to do it.
（為了國家的利益，我勢必要這樣做。）

例 I must do it right away.
（我得馬上開始做。）

【情況會話 2】 *********************

John: I don't know how Frank will make it without a job. He is a big spender.
（我不知道法蘭克沒有工作要怎樣活下去？他花錢很凶的。）

Julie: Well, now he doesn't have a job. He has to cut back on his spending.
（他現在沒工作了，得緊縮開支了。）

▶ **make it:** 活下去，做成功，度得過

例 Do you think he can make it?
(你認為他可以做得成嗎？)

例 The doctor wants the family to be prepared.
Grandpa may not make it.
(醫生叫全家人要有心理準備，爺爺也許沒希
望了。)

▶ **a big spender:** 花錢很凶

例 I had to break with my girlfriend. She was
a big spender. I couldn't afford.
(我只好和我女朋友分手。她花錢好凶，我負
擔不起。)

UNIT 31

CUT IT OUT

（得了吧，不要再說了。）

說明

　　當別人對著你一陣疲勞轟炸，說的盡是你不愛聽的事，叫他不要再說了，很多人可能不自覺的用 shut up，偏偏 shut up 在美國小學裡是禁用語之一，原因是不夠禮貌，有閉上你的烏鴉嘴的意思。還是用 cut it out 吧，在熟人之間聽起來較親切。

【情況會話 1】 **********************

John: Hey, Julie. Can you loan me some money?
（嗨，茱莉，可以借我一些錢嗎？）

Julie: Cut it out, John. Don't even think about it.
（不用再說了，門都沒有。）

　　cut 是截斷，it 是指正在說的事，out 是中斷。cut it out 合起來是將正在說的事到此為止，不要再說下去了。

【相關語彙】

▶ **loan:** 貸款。華人常用 borrow some money，這有點洋涇濱。美語中 borrow 是指借東西用，借錢一般都用 loan，跟銀行或個人週轉，數額多少都沒有關係。

例 I am out of cash. Would you loan me a few dollars?
（我身上沒有現金，借我幾塊錢好嗎？）

例 Can I borrow your pen?
（可以借用你的筆嗎？）

▶ **Don't even think about it.:** 門都沒有。要對方想都別想，死心的意思。

例 I know what you want, but don't even think about it.
（我知道你想幹什麼，但最好早點死心，想都不要想。）

【情況會話 2】 ✳✳✳✳✳✳✳✳✳✳✳✳✳✳✳✳✳✳✳✳✳

John: How about going to a movie tonight, Julie?
（今晚去看場電影如何？）

Julie: Cut it out, John. I told you I am not going.
（得了吧，約翰。跟你說我不去。）

【相關語彙】

▶ **How about:** 來做某事如何，給別人建議時用。

例 How about going to lunch sometime this week?
（這星期找個時間一起吃午餐如何？）

例 A: I can't make it this week.
（我這星期不行。）

B: Then, how about next week?
（那下星期行不行？）

UNIT 32

GO FIFTY-FIFTY

（五五對分；各付各的）

說明

有些人學的英語較老式，永遠以為各付各的叫 go dutch，拿著對美國人一直用。姑且不論這種話是不是歧視荷蘭人，像蒙古大夫一詞有歧視蒙古的意味。現代人說美語，就要有個現代氣息，go fifty-fifty，清楚扼要，多麼好用！

【情況會話 1】 ***********************

John: Let's go to lunch. I'll pay for you.
（我們去吃午餐，我請妳。）

Julie: Thank you. But I prefer going fifty-fifty.
（謝了，我寧願各付各的。）

fifty-fifty 比較容易記，go 原意是去某個地方，在這裡是採用某種方法。go fifty-fifty 指採用五五對分，各付各的。

【相關語彙】

▶ **pay for:** 付錢。for 的後面接東西時，指東西的價錢。

例 How much did you pay for your house?
（你的房子多少錢買的？）

▶ **prefer:** 比較喜歡，記得接動詞時要加 ing。

例 I prefer seeing you in the office.
（我比較喜歡跟你在辦公室會面。）

【情況會話 2】 ***********************

John: I want to move out of my dad's house, but I can't afford to rent an apartment.
（我想搬出我老爸的房子，可是負擔不起租公寓的錢。）

Julie: Well, maybe you can find a roommate and share the apartment by going fifty-fifty.
（或許你可以找個室友，兩個人一起分擔房租。）

▶ **move out:** 搬出去

　例 I plan to move out to a new apartment next month.
（我計劃下個月搬到另一間新公寓。）

▶ **roommate:** 同住一間公寓或房間的室友。

　例 My roommate is moving out, but I am staying.
（我室友要搬出去，可是我要留下來。）

▶ **by:** 意思很多。這裡指使用某種方法。

　例 I went to Shanghai by train.
（我坐火車到上海。）

UNIT 33

MP3-34

DO AWAY WITH
（消除，不再使用）

說明

　　儘管有幾個英語單字和詞彙可以表達消除，或放棄的意思，但論簡單易記又好用，就數 do away with 了。以台灣英語課本來看，國中一年級就學過這三個字。再參照下面的會話，你的英語會話能力，馬上功力大增。

【情況會話 1】 *********************

Julie: American women are going back to nature. A lot of them are doing away with make-ups.
（美國女性正在回歸自然，許多人都不再使用化粧品。）

John: A lot of Chinese women are not using make-ups in the first place.

（很多中國女性根本就不用化粧品。）

do 是做，away 是弄走，with 是指對象。三個合起來 do away with 當然就是把某種東西或人給清除掉。

【相關語彙】

▶ **go back to nature:** 回歸自然。

例 Going back to nature is a way to improve health.

（回歸自然是改善健康的一個方法。）

▶ **make-up:** 化粧品。

例 American girls like to wear make-up.

（美國女孩喜歡化粧。）

【情況會話２】

John: I had a horrible dream last night that some bad guys were trying to do away with Frank.
（我昨晚做了個恐怖的夢，有幾個壞人要做掉法蘭克。）

Julie: You mean to kill Frank?
（你是說殺他？）

John: Yes.
（是的。）

【相關語彙】

▶ **horrible:** 恐佈。許多人將這個字與 terrible 弄混淆，horrible 指心裡會怕的東西，terrible 是很糟糕，糟得可怕，但不是真的恐佈。

例 The ghost story he told was horrible. It scared us so much.
（他講的鬼故事好恐怖，把我們嚇得半死。）

例 The ghost story he told was terrible. No one believed him and no one was scared.
（他講的鬼故事糟透了，沒人相信他也沒人害怕。）

MP3-35

DO BETTER THAN THAT

（我對你的表現不太滿意）

說明

中美文化差異在語言上充分表現出來。同樣是對別人的表現不滿意，華人可能很直接的指責，而美國人說你可以做得更好。對學英語的人來說，這類的美式表達方式一定要會，否則不僅挖空心思把自己的意思一一翻譯，還是不能叫美國人聽懂，有時在措詞上得罪對方，壞了整個生意談判，還不知道問題出在那裡呢！

【情況會話 1 】 **********************

（時間到，John 的試題沒寫完。）

John: Here you are, ma'am. I didn't finish it.
（交給妳，老師。我沒寫完。）

Teacher: I am surprised, John. I thought you
would do better than that.
（我很驚訝，我認為你的表現會更好的。）

這句話指你應該可以做得更好，整句一次記起來最
好。You can do better than that.

【相關語彙】

▶ **Here you are.:** 拿東西給別人時用。

例 Here you are, John. Is this what you want?
（拿去，約翰。這就是你要的東西嗎？）

▶ **ma'am:** 稱女士或地位較高的女人時用。對男士用 Sir。
這兩個字與 Yes 和 No 聯用，可增加對方好感，使你獲得對
方合作的機會大增，注意聽 MP3 的語調。

例 Yes, ma'am.

No, sir.

Thank you, ma'am.

I'll open the door for you, sir.

Be careful, ma'am.

所有以上的例句中，sir 和 ma'am 都是表示客氣加上
去的。

【情況會話 2】 *********************

Julie: When can you get it done and give it to me?
（你幾時可以做好交給我？）

John: I think I need one month to do it.
（我想我需要一個月時間。）

Julie: Come on, you can do better than that.
（算了吧，你要那麼久啊！）

【情況會話 3】

John: The price is too high. Can you cut it back a little?
（價格太貴了，能不能便宜一點？）

Julie: Well, I can give you a 5 percent discount.
（這樣吧，我給你打九五折。）

John: Come-on, you can do better than that.
（唉，太少了吧！）

【相關語彙】

▶ **cut the price:** 減價。

例 This is the best buy for you. I can't cut the price any more.
(對你而言，這已是最好的買賣，我不能再減價了。)

▶ **5 percent discount:** 九五折。美式折扣說法是講扣多少百分比。扣百分之五就是九五折。

例 5 percent discount is not good enough. I want at least a 20 percent discount.
(九五折還不夠好。我要最少打八折才買。)

FISH OR CUT BAIT

（要就好好做，不要就拉倒。）

說明

　　天下父母心，中國長輩與上司最喜歡用這句話來「鼓舞」後進了。此外，在時間就是金錢的時代裡，效率第一，任何公司要有利潤，所有員工都要 fish or cut bait.

【情況會話 1】 ********************

（老爸對女兒的成績不滿意。）

Father: With your grades now, I don't see how you can pass the college entrance exam. I want you to fish or cut bait. Stop wasting time.
（以你現在的成績，我看不出妳可以考上大學，妳要不就好好唸書，不然就趁早算了，別浪費時間。）

Daughter: I'm trying, Dad. Plus, my grade is
much better than last time.
(爸,我一直在努力。何況,我的成績比上回
好很多。)

　　fish 是釣魚,or 是否則,cut bait 是切斷魚餌。合
起來指好好釣魚,否則就切斷魚餌別釣了。

【相關語彙】

▶ **I don't see how you can:** 我不認為你可以。

例 I don't see how you can open a can without
an opener.
(我不認為你可以不用開罐器打開罐頭。)

▶ **plus:** 何況,plus 不僅是加的意思。美語中的何況用 plus
非常自然生動。

例 I quit smoking. It's not good to my health.
And plus, it's getting expensive.
(我戒煙了。抽煙對健康不好,更何況香煙越
來越貴。)

【情況會話 2】 ***********************

John: I think Frank is doing a much better job now.
（我看法蘭克現在工作表現比較好了。）

Julie: Yes, after his boss told him to fish or cut bait.
（是啊，在他主管叫他要就好好做，不做就拉倒之後。）

【相關語彙】

▶ **do a better job:** 工作表現比較好。

例 The new secrectary in my office is doing a better job now.
（我辦公室裡的女秘書現在工作表現比較好了。）

▶ **Boss:** 頂頭上司。

例 My boss is a good guy.
（我主管是個好人。）

PART IV

UNIT 36

FROM THE HEART

（真心誠意的）

說明

　　人與人之間講究真誠以待，無論是道謝或道歉，都應該 from the heart。美語中用 heart 表達的語句很多，都指著感情方面而言，非理性的，但是可以體會得出來的。

【情況會話 1】 ********************

John: Why did you reject his gifts?
（妳怎麼不接受他的禮物？）

Julie: Because I don't think it was from the heart.
（因為我不認為那出自真心。）

from the heart 來自內心，當然是出於真誠的了。

【相關語彙】

▶ **have a heart:** 仁慈一些。

　　例 Come on, guys. Have a heart. Let's give these homeless some help.
（來吧，朋友們。仁慈一些，我們來給這些無家可歸的人一些幫助吧。）

▶ **break someone's heart:** 傷人的心。

　　例 The news that their daughter failed in the college extrance exam broke their heart.
（女兒沒考上大學的消息，讓他們很傷心。）

▶ **cross one's heart:** 發誓所言都是實在的，像美國法庭上的發誓，以手抱胸。

　　例 Frank did not do it. I cross my heart.
（我發誓。那不是法蘭克做的。）

【情況會話 2】 ********************

John: When I say something nice about you,
count on it. I don't tell white lies.
（我說妳好話的時候，相信我。我不說善意的謊言。）

Julie: I believe you. Your nice words come from
the heart.
（我相信你，你的甜言蜜語皆是真心誠意的。）

【相關語彙】

▶ **count on it.:** 可以相信它，毋庸置疑，美語說法很普遍的一句。

例 Count on it. David will be late. He never
does anything on time.
（不用懷疑，大衛一定遲到。他做事從來都不準時。）

▶ **white lie:** 善意的謊言。指所言不實，但卻是出自一片好意才撒謊。

例 I had to tell white lies. The truth might
break their heart.
（我必須善意的撒謊，因為實話可能會讓他們傷心。）

UNIT 37

GET AWAY FROM IT ALL

（把工作雜事拋在腦後）

說明

工商社會，天天繁忙。要是能將工作雜事拋在腦後，將是多麼輕鬆的事。美國人常渡假旅行，台灣很多人上山朝拜，無非都是要 get away from it all.

【情況會話 1】 *************************

John: How was your vacation?
（妳的假期過得好嗎？）

Julie: Too short. Oh, it was so good to get away from it all.
（太短了。噢！能把一切拋諸腦後真好。）

get away 是逃開，from it all 指放下所有的東西，
所以合起來就是放下雜務不管，求個清閒。在美語中，
一般用在工作場合，特別在渡假的話題上。

【相關語彙】

▶ **vacation:** 年假、長假。當美國人問你有關 vacation
時，注意他不是在問新年、端午節一類的放假，那些叫
holidays，他在問你的年休假。

例 I used all my vacation days.
（我的年休假全都休完了。）

▶ **too short:** 太短了。當別人問起你的假日、週末旅遊一
類的事，不要只會用 very good 這類沒英語水準的話來回
答，用這句 too short，表示好得不得了，只可惜太短促了。

例 A: How was your weekend?
（週末過得好嗎？）

B: Too short.
（好啊，只是太短促了。）

【情況會話 2】 ********************

Husband: Honey, my vacation is coming up in
two weeks. Do you have anywhere in

mind that you prefer to go?
(太太，再過兩星期我就休年假，你心裡有沒有打算去那裡玩？)

Wife: Not really. Just a place that you can get away from it all.
(沒有。只要是一個你可以拋開一切的地方就行。)

【相關語彙】

▶ **coming up:** 接著就要來的。

例 I can't go to the movie. My final is coming up.
(我不能去看電影，期末考就要到了。)

▶ **Not really:** 是 No 的意思。但說起來帶一點淡淡的口吻，注意聽 MP3 的表情。

例 A: I am going to the United States next week. Do you want me to bring anything back for you.
(下星期我要去美國。你要我幫你帶些什麼東西回來嗎？)

B: No, not really.
(不用了，沒什麼。)

UNIT 38

 MP3-39

HANG ON

（緊緊抓住）

說明

　　動作片裡，經常看到這類驚險鏡頭，就是男主角和女主角開車準備加油衝殺，男主角說 hang on，牢牢坐好；泰山救美，一手握著樹藤，一手抱住美人說 hang on，抱緊了。現實社會用到 hang on 也很多，這裡有好幾個不同的情況都用了這個詞。

【情況會話 1】 ***********************

(老公對老婆。)

Husband: I am so afraid that I might lose my
job. The company is cutting back on
staff.
（我很怕丟了工作，公司正在裁員。）

Wife:　　Don't worry, honey. Just hang on to the job and start looking for something else.

（別擔心。暫時佔著這個工作，然後騎驢找馬。）

　　hang 是懸掛，on 是在東西上。合起來就是吊在東西上面，指牢牢抓緊。hang on to 是抓緊 to 後面所接的名詞。

【相關語彙】

▶ **lose one's job:** 失去工作。

　例 Don't worry that you may lose your job as long as you are doing a good job on it.
（只要你表現好，就不要擔心失去工作。）

▶ **look for:** 找。

　例 My dog ran away the other day. I have been looking for it.
（我的狗前幾天走失了。我一直在找它。）

【情況會話 2】 *******************

(在擁擠的百貨公司裡。)

Julie: It's too crowded here today.
（今天這裡太擠了。）

John: Yes. You've got to hang on to your purse. It might get stolen.
（是呀，看緊你的皮包，小心被扒。）

Julie: O.K. I will.
（好，我會的。）

【相關語彙】

▸ **crowded:** 擁擠。

例 Taipei is a crowded city.
（台北是一個擁擠的都市。）

▸ **get stolen:** 被偷了、丟了。美語有一些字喜歡用被動式，這是一個例子。

例 He was really down because his car got stolen.
（他的車被人偷了，所以他心情很差。）

【情況會話 **3**】 **********************

(克林頓總統的故事對 John 的啟發。)

John: I read a story about Bill Clinton and I learned something important.
(我讀到一則有關克林頓總統的故事，學到了很重要的事。)

Julie: What was it?
(學到什麼？)

John: He made up his mind to be the president of the United States when he was 16. And he made it.
(他 16 歲就決心要成為美國總統。他做到了。)

Julie: So? What did you learn from it?
(那，你到底學到什麼？)

John: When you have a idea, hang on to it, try your best and you will make it.
(當你有個理想，緊抓著它，努力去做，一定會有成功的一天。)

▶ **make up one's mind:** 下定決心。

例 I made up my mind to take vacation and
get away from it all.
(我下定決心要休年假,把一切雜事丟在腦後。)

▶ **So?:** 那又如何,期待下文的意思。有時是覺得沒什麼大不
了的事而說的。

例 A: He got himself hurt.
(他受傷了。)

B: So?
(那又如何?有什麼大不了?)

UNIT 39

HIT BOTTOM
（達到谷底，否極泰來）

　　物極必反。不論談什麼事，從國家經濟到個人成績，會說 hit bottom 是很要緊的。特別是公開場合，有人談到諸事不順，你及時地回答他已經 hit bottom，就要 get better，一定會叫那人感激地引你為知音的。

【情況會話 1】 ********************

John: Our company is not making money. I might lose my job.
（我們公司不賺錢。我也許會失業。）

Julie: Be positive. I think it has already hit bottom. Things will change.
（樂觀一點，我想你公司已經壞到谷底，就要有轉機了。）

hit 原意是打擊到某一點，這裡是達到的意思，bottom 是最底端。所以 hit bottom 就是達到最低點，要回升了。

【相關語彙】

▶ **be positive:** 樂觀一點。用在祈使句，單獨使用，例如說某人是 positive，則指很確定。

　例 Be positive. Things will get better.
　　（樂觀一點。事情會變好。）

　例 I am positive that Frank is going to be fired.
　　（我很確定法蘭克要被炒魷魚。）

▶ **things will change.:** 安慰別人時用的話。指事情會有轉機。

　例 You must feel no way out now, but things will change.
　　（你一定覺得無路可走，但事情總會有轉機的。）

【情況會話 2】 **********************

(父親對女兒。)

Father: Your grades seems to be getting worse and worse. When are you going to hit bottom and become better.
（你的成績越來越差。妳幾時才會到谷底回升？）

Daughter: I am trying my best, Dad.
（我一直在努力唸書，爸爸。）

【相關語彙】

▶ **get worse and worse:** 變得越來越差。

例 The weather is getting worse and worse. Let's call it a day early.
（天氣越來越壞，我們今天早點收工吧。）

▶ **try one's best:** 盡力而為。

例 Remember this, whatever you do, try your best.
（記住。做任何事都要盡力而為。）

【情況會話 3】 ＊＊＊＊＊＊＊＊＊＊＊＊＊＊＊＊＊＊＊＊＊

John: When the stock market hits bottom, it's time to buy. You'll make a lot of money.
（當股市跌到谷底，就是買進的時候。你一定可以賺很多錢。）

Julie: I agree. But the question is, how do you know it's the bottom.
（我同意。但問題是，你怎樣知道是不是已經跌到谷底？）

【相關語彙】

▶ **it's time to:** 是做某事的時間了。

例 Children, it's time to go to bed.
（孩子們，睡覺時間到了。）

▶ **it's high time to:** 做某事的最佳時機。是上一句的加強用語。

例 It's high time to pull out from Somalia.
（是從索馬利亞撤出的時機了。）

GOOD-FOR-NOTHING
（窩囊廢。啥事都不會幹。）

說明

人常常有優越感，所以經常就要有人抱怨被輕視。當別人瞧我們一文不值的時候，我們如何來形容他的態度呢？ good-for-nothing 是最容易又清楚的說法了。

【情況會話 1】 ＊＊＊＊＊＊＊＊＊＊＊＊＊＊＊＊＊＊＊＊＊

(坐在車上，邊開車邊聊天。)

John: My car is good for nothing. It breaks down every other day.
（我的車真是一無是處。每兩天故障一次。）

Julie: It's old.
（老古董了！）

good 大家都知道是好的意思，for nothing 是什麼事都不要或不會。合起來就是什麼事都做不好。

【相關語彙】

▶ **break down:** 車子拋錨。

例 My car broke down on the highway today.
（我的車今天在高速公路上拋錨。）

▶ **every other day:** 每隔一天，即兩天一次的意思。

例 He is very ill. He needs to visit the hospital every other day.
（他病得很厲害，每兩天要上一次醫院。）

【情況會話 2】 ******************

(說長道短)

Julie: Mrs. Lee is always complaining about her husband. He treats her like she is good-for-nothing.
（李太太老是在埋怨他先生。他從不把她當作一回事。）

John: If he is so bad, how come she is still hanging on to him?
（他要是那麼差，為何她還要跟他在一起？）

【相關語彙】

▶ **treat someone like dirt:** 把人當做窩囊廢的另一種最常說的英語說法。dirt 原意是泥土。

　　例 Mr. Lee treats his wife like dirt.
　　　（李先生對她太太好像她是窩囊廢。）

▶ **how come:** 為什麼，與 why 同意。但用 how come 時，主詞、動詞習慣上不對調。

　　例 Why is he not coming?
　　　（他怎麼不來？）

　　　How come he is not coming?
　　　（他怎麼不來。）

▶ **hang on to:** 緊緊抓住。參照 UNIT 38。

【情況會話 3】 *************************

(在辦公室裡。)

Julie: The secretary in my office is good-for-nothing. She always makes mistakes. It seems she can never get anything done right.

(我辦公室的秘書啥事都不會。她老犯錯誤，好像從沒做對一件事。)

John: I told you she was new. Give her some time. She will improve.

(我告訴過妳她是新來的。給她一點時間，會進步的。)

【相關語彙】

▶ **can never:** 永遠都不會。

　例 You can never be too careful.
　　(謹慎一點不算過分 [還是小心一點好]。)

▶ **get something done right:** 做對某件事。

　例 Now, watch me real good. Next time, you've got to get it done right by yourself.
　　(現在仔細看我做。下回你要自己把它做對了。)

GO THROUGH

（從頭到尾；通過法律）

說明

　　go throught 意思很多。美語日常生活中最常表示從頭到尾看過或討論過一次的意思。用 go through 就不要用生硬的 from the begining to the end 或 through the end。通過某條法律，也叫 go through。

【情況會話 1】 ****************************

John: Is there a way to get better grades? I have try very hard but it seems not to be working.

（有沒有辦法提高成績？我努力嘗試但似乎徒勞無功。）

Julie: Well, maybe you need to improve your skills in test. Before you turn in your tests, always go through the answer one more time.
（那也許你須改善你的考試技巧。在交卷之前，一定要把答案從頭到尾再檢查一次。）

　　go 是去或走的意思，through 是整個貫穿。所以 go through 是從頭到尾來一次的意思。也可以當做法律經過層層審核，終告通過。

【 相關語彙 】

▶ **not working:** 無效。

　囫 I've tried a lot of different ways. None of them are working.
　　（我試過好多方法，沒一樣有效的。）

▶ **turn in:** 繳交。

　囫 I'm glad I turned in my report on time.
　　（我很高興我準時交了報告。）

【情況會話 2】 ******************

John: When your paper is done, go through it again and make sure there are no misspelled words.
（當你完成書面報告，從頭到尾檢查一次，要確定沒有拼錯字。）

Julie: I use a word processor to do my paper, and it has check spelling function. I won't have any misspelled words.
（我的報告是用文書處理軟體打的，它有檢測拼字的功能。我絕不會有誤拼的字。）

【相關語彙】

▶ **paper:** 在學校場合裡，指書面報告或論文。

例 We have to do 3 papers in one month.
（我們一個月內要寫出三篇論文。）

▶ **word processor:** 打字用的電腦文書處理軟體。

例 How come you are still using a typewriter? Everybody else is using word processors now.
（你怎麼還用打字機呢？別人都用文書處理軟體了。）

【情況會話 3】 ************************

John: A new law went through today. It requires all car owners to buy parking space for their car.
（今天通過一條新法律，要求每個汽車所有人都要自備一個停車位。）

Julie: Wow, who can afford it?
（噢，誰買得起啊？）

【相關語彙】

▸ **parking space:** 停車位。與 UNIT 13 裡的 parking lot 不同。後者是停車場。

例 You can hardly find a parking space in Taipei.
（在台北幾乎找不到一個停車位。）

例 There is a parking lot in front of the building.
（大樓前面有個停車場。）

▸ **parking garage:** 地下或立體室內停車場。注意聽 MP3 裡 garage 的發音。

例 There is no parking garage in this building.
（這棟大樓沒有地下停車場。）

UNIT 42

HAVE A SAY IN SOMETHING

（參與決策）

說明

　　民主社會人人都要參與決策，連家裡的小霸王也不再安於有耳無嘴的傳統身份，要對父母提出種種要求。不要把英語想得太難是本書一直強調的。have a say in something 或 anything，那個字不是國中一年級就學過的單字呢？這幾個小字合起來就是參與決策的意思了。

【情況會話 1】　*********************

Julie:　My husband treats me like I am good for nothing?
（我先生把我看作一點用處都沒有。）

John: How come?
（怎麼說？）

Julie: He is always the one that makes the
decisions. I have no say in anything.
（做決定的永遠是他。我根本不能參與決策。）

Have a say 是有發言權，in something 是在某件事
上。二句合起來，對某件事有發言權，就是參與決策，
用在否定句裡，沒有決策權，就是 not have a say in
anything.

【相關語彙】

▶ **make the decisions:** 下決策。

例 A good leader knows when to make the
decisions.
（好的領導人知道什麼時候該下決策。）

【情況會話 2】 *************************

John: I can't stand my boss.
（我受不了我的老闆。）

Julie: Why?
（為什麼？）

John: He likes to show he is the one who carries the ball. No other person has a say in anything.
（他很喜歡表現他是主導人物。其他人一概不能參與決策。）

【相關語彙】

▶ **can't stand:** 不能忍受，後面可以接人或接事物。

例 I can't stand the noise day after day. I need to move to somewhere else.
（我受不了每天的噪音。我得搬到別的地方。）

▶ **like to:** 喜歡做某件事，強調做的動作。若是強調喜歡的事，用 like 之後直接加動名詞。

例 I like to play golf this afternoon.
（我今天下午想打高爾夫球。）

I like playing golf in Beijing.
（我喜歡在北京打高爾夫球。）

【情況會話 3】　********************

Julie: Time is changing and children are changing, too.
（時代在變，小孩也在變。）

John: What is that?
（怎麼說？）

John: It used to be the children do what the parents want them to do. Now, the children want a say in everything.
（從前是小孩做父母要他們做的事。現在，小孩事事要參與決策。）

【相關語彙】

▶ **Time is changing.:** 時代在變。

例 Time is changing. It's O.K. for girls to hang out late.
（時代在變。女孩在外面待晚一點也沒關係。）

▶ **used to:** 從前一直是。

例 I used to skip the breakfast.
（我從前一直是不吃早餐的。）

UNIT 43

MP3-44

IN BLACK AND WHITE

（白紙寫黑字、證據確鑿）

說明

　　black and white 很多人知道是黑白的意思，如黑白電影、黑白電視，多加一個 in 就可以表示白紙寫黑字，證據明確。許多人迷信記英文單字，實際上，幾萬個單字記下來，不會用是浪費時間。像 in black and white 這種不費吹灰之力就可以活學活用的字，才是最應該知道的。

【情況會話 1】　＊＊＊＊＊＊＊＊＊＊＊＊＊＊＊＊＊＊＊＊＊

（談商業契約。）

John: Before you sign the paper, be sure to go through it again.

（在簽文件之前，要確實從頭到尾再看一遍。）

Julie: Yes, I know. After you sign it, it is in black and white. You can't change it.

（好，我知道。簽字之後，就是白紙黑字，更改不得的。）

in black and white，不用任何記憶法，你已經記得了。它指白紙黑字，不能更改。

【相關語彙】

▶ **sign the paper:** 商場上，用到簽名的 paper，一定是文件。與 UNIT 41 的 paper 意思不同。

例 Have your father sign the paper. You are under age.

（叫你父親簽文件，你還未成年。）

【情況會話 2】 **************************

(洽談生意。)

Julie: Sorry to tell you this, but I have to reconsider the deal we talked about the other day.
（抱歉告訴你這件事。我們前幾天所談的生意我得重新考慮。）

John: Wait a minute, you have signed the contract. It is in black and white, you can't back out now.
（慢著，你簽了合同。白紙黑字，你不能不認賬。）

【 相關語彙 】

▶ **reconsider the deal:** 重新考慮一筆生意。

　　例 I wish you reconsider the deal.
　　　（我希望你重新考慮這筆生意。）

▶ **talk about:** 商談或談論。

　　例 I don't know what you are talking about.
　　　（我不懂你在說什麼。）

【情況會話 3】 **********************

(商談。)

John: In a court, you can't argue without something in black and white.
(在法庭上，沒有確鑿的證據是不能辯論的。)

Julie: Yes, that's why we need to make it a habit to keep records.
(是的。那就是為什麼要養成保留文件的習慣。)

【相關語彙】

▶ **In a court, in the court:** 法庭上。

例 Food and drink are not allowed in the court.
(法庭上不準吃東西。)

▶ **that's why:** 那就是為什麼。

例 My boss is very picky. That's why I do everything very carefully.
(我的主管很挑剔。那就是為什麼我做事都很小心。)

▶ **keep records:** 保留文件做為記錄。

例 The secretary keeps records in the office.
(秘書替辦公室的人保留文件記錄。)

MP3-45

JUMP ON SOMEONE
(大發雷霆，大發脾氣)

說明

　　許多人一想到生氣，就只會用 angry，其實 angry 只表示憤怒、不高興，所以當一個人對你 angry，他可以不理你。若是他搶到你面前，指著你鼻子開罵，那他就不是 angry 而是 jump on 你了。

【情況會話 1】 *******************

(吐露悶氣。)

John: The other night I went home too late. My dad jumped on me real bad.
(前幾天晚上，我太晚回家。我老爸著實對我發了一頓脾氣。)

Julie: Then, next time be sure to go home early. Don't hang out too late.

（那，下次早點回家。不要在外逗留太晚。）

　　大發雷霆，中國的話可以說是暴跳如雷。jump 是跳的意思，jump on 是往別人身上跳，和跳腳意思是一樣的。

【相關語彙】

▶ **the other night:** 前幾天晚上。

例 We were going to a movie the other night, but the tickets were sold out.
（前幾天晚上，我們去看電影，但票全部賣光了。）

▶ **real bad:** 非常。

例 I need some money real bad.
（我非常需要錢。）

【情況會話 2】 *******************

John: My mother jumped on me because someone broke her favorite vase.
（我媽媽對我大發脾氣，因為有人打破她最心愛的花瓶。）

Julie: Did you do it?
（是你打破的嗎？）

John: I wasn't even home when it happened.
（事情發生時，我根本不在家。）

【相關語彙】

▶ **favorite:** 最喜愛的。

例 Sharon Stone is my favorite movie star.
（莎朗史東是我最喜愛的明星。）

▶ **not even:** 根本，連 ....。作加強語氣用。

例 You missed by a mile. That was not even close.
（你差了十萬八千里，連邊都沾不上。）

【情況會話 3】 *********************

John: Frank did something to tick my boss off.
He jumped on Frank today in the office.
（法蘭克做了什麼事惹火了我老闆。他今天在辦公室對法蘭克大發脾氣。）

Julie: He didn't fire Frank, did he?
（他沒開除法蘭克，是嗎？）

John: No, not really. But for a moment, I thought
he was going to.
（沒有。可是有一剎那，我以為他會。）

【相關語彙】

▸ **tick someone off:** 惹火某人。

例 He is a punk. His hair style ticks me off.
（他是個龐客族 [混混]。那一頭髮型真惹火我。）

▸ **for a moment:** 有一剎那時間。

例 He was so sick. For a moment, I thought he
was dying.
（他病得好重。有一剎那時間，我覺得他就要死了。）

A FAR CRY

（差得很遠）

説明

　　與事實或預計的事差得很遠，不要用 far from，用 far cry from，因為 far from 是指距離而言，而 far cry 是用做比喻，兩者不要混淆。

【情況會話 1】 ********************

（商談。）

John: I had to return the whole shipment I ordered. The quality of the goods was a far cry from the sample.
（我必須把訂的貨整批退貨。那批貨品的品質和樣本差得太遠了。）

Julie: I hear you. Sometimes businessmen tend to cut corners.
（我瞭解。生意人有時會偷工減料。）

far 是遙遠，cry 是叫聲。野地裡野獸的叫聲很遙遠，這裡借來引申為一點都不接近重點。

【相關語彙】

▶ **shipment:** 交貨。

例 It's a big order. We need to separate it into three shipments.
（那是個大訂單。我們必須分成三批交貨。）

▶ **tend to:** 有某種傾向。

例 People tend to buy in the bull market.
（股票漲的時候，人們喜歡追買。）

【情況會話 2】 ************************

(在咖啡廳。)

John: Frank can't play the piano. I think he is all thumbs.
（法蘭克不會彈鋼琴。我看他是笨手笨腳。）

Julie: You are right. What he played was a far cry from what I call music.
（你說得對。他彈的與我所想像的音樂差太遠。）

【相關語彙】

▸ **You are right.:** 你說得對。

　　例 You are right. It's too crowded in Nanjing.
　　（你說得對。南京真的太擁擠了。）

▸ **what I call:** 我所想像的。

　　例 What I call a model worker is not like him.
　　（我想像中的勞工楷模不是像他那樣。）

【情況會話 **3**】　**********************

(在辦公室中。)

John:　Why did you reject his gifts?
　　　　（你為什麼拒絕他的禮物？）

Julie:　I expected something from the heart. But
　　　　from the way he handed it to me, it was a
　　　　far cry from that.
　　　　（我期待真心好禮。可是從他送東西給我的態度
　　　　來看，差得太遠了。）

▶ **the way:** 某種方法或態度

例 The way you talked to your boss was wrong.
（你對你老闆說話的態度不對。）

UNIT 46

KISS SOMETHING GOOD-BYE

（徹底把事物遺忘）

說明

吻別是大家都知道的，可是 kiss something good-bye 不是吻了然後明天再見，而是永遠不再提起。是叫人徹底放棄一個念頭的意思。

【情況會話1】 ********************

（約翰自怨自艾地。）

John: Time and things are changing.
（時代和事物都在變遷。）

Julie: What is it?
（又怎麼啦？）

John: It used to be that, if you left something somewhere, you could still find it or someone might return it to you. But now you can kiss it good-bye.

（從前是，你要是在某個地方遺留東西，你還可以找到，或者別人會還給你。現在，你可以徹底把它給忘了。）

　　會唱「吻別」這首歌的人，一定可以記住 kiss something good-bye，永遠地忘記。

【相關語彙】

▶ **somewhere:** 某個地方。

　例 I remember I saw my purse somewhere.
　　（我記得在那裡看過我的皮包。）

【情況會話 2】 *********************

（在家裡）

Julie: I hope someone will find my lost ring and return it to me.
（我希望有人會撿到我弄丟的戒指還給我。）

John: Honey, it's been a couple of weeks since you lost it. You had better kiss it good-bye.
（老婆，你掉了戒指已經兩星期了，最好忘了吧！）

【相關語彙】

▶ **a couple of:** 指期間，一般是兩個的意思。指東西也可以指兩、三個不太確定的數目。

例 Can you loan me a couple of dollars?
（借我兩三塊錢，好嗎？）

▶ **had better:** 最好。

例 You had better turn in your paper on time, otherwise I am not going to grade it.
（你最好按時交你的報告，否則我不給予評分。）

UP FRONT

（首付；頭期款）

說明

分期付款購物，已經很普遍。一般都有個頭期款，到底英語該怎麼說呢？若是專指頭期款，可以用 down payment。可是還有個更口語的說法，涵蓋面更廣，叫 up front，通稱首付款。

【情況會話 1】 ********************

(在路上。)

Julie: Want to have a look at my new car?
（要看看我的新車嗎？）

John: Wow, it's a nice car. How much did you pay for it?
（哇，好車。多少錢買的？）

Julie: 5,000 dollars up front and 250 dollars a month.
（首付五千元，每個月再付 250 元。）

　　up 有直到面前的意思，front 是起頭或面前。up front 合起來是在開頭之前，所以是預先（首付）的意思。

【相關語彙】

▶ **have a look at:** 看看。

例 Let me have a look at your new dress.
（讓我看看你的新衣服。）

【情況會話 2】 ✻✻✻✻✻✻✻✻✻✻✻✻✻✻✻✻✻✻✻✻✻✻

（在家裡。）

Julie: How do you charge for fixing my air conditioner?
（修我的冷氣機要收多少錢？）

John: The total charge is 20,000 dollars. You may pay 5,000 up front, and when the job is done, pay me the rest.
（全部費用兩萬元。你可以預付五千，等完工再付我其餘的。）

▶ **How do you charge for:** 怎麼算我錢？收我多少錢？等於 How much is it to。

例 How do you charge for towing my car?

How much is it to tow my car?
(幫我拖車要收多少錢？)

▶ **total charge:** 總價。

例 The total charge is 10,000 dollars. But I'll give you a 5 percent discount.
(總價一萬元。我給你打 95 折。)

【情況會話 3】 ***********************

(購屋。)

Julie: I like the house very much, but I am afraid I can't afford it.
(我很喜歡這間房子，但我怕負擔不起。)

John: Yes, you can. Look, the up front payment is just 50,000 dollars. Your monthly payment if you get a loan for 30 years, will be low enough for you to afford.
(沒問題，你負擔得起。喏，頭期款只有五萬元，要是你貸款三十年，每個月的付款就會很少，你付得起。)

【相關語彙】

▶ **up front payment:** 頭期款，等於 down payment.

例 I bought my car without a down payment.
（我免付頭期款買了我的車。）

▶ **Look:** 說話時起頭語，沒特別的意思。約等於「喏」。

例 Look, you had better leave me alone before I call the police.
（喏，在我報警之前，你最好別再煩我。）

UNIT 48

MAKE A COMEBACK
（東山再起）

說明

　　拿這句做本書最後一句話，最好不過了。很多人在讀本書之前，對英語一定深感挫折，現學現忘。讀了本書之後，你發現只要有好的書，好的方法，英語是很簡單的。用你中學裡的單字，就可以應付天文地理，讀了本文之後，你就可以大呼 I am making a comeback in speaking English.（我東山再起，會說英文了！）

【情況會話 1】 ********************

（在客廳）

John: More and more people give up soft drink and drink tea.
（愈來愈多人不喝汽水，改喝茶。）

Julie: Yes, after several years of low sales, tea is making a comeback.
(是的。過了幾年的清淡生意之後,茶的銷售額又東山再起了。)

come back 是回來的意思,兩字合成一字,comeback 是指回來這件事。make a comeback 就是去了,又回來,引申為東山再起。

【相關語彙】

▶ **soft drink:** 汽水,軟性飲料。

例 Kids at large love soft drink.
(絕大部分的小孩愛喝汽水。)

▶ **low sales:** 銷售不佳。

例 Because of the low sales, the company had to cut back on staff.
(因為銷售不佳,這家公司需要裁員。)

【情況會話 2】 ************************

(在咖啡廳。)

John: In business world, you've got to be very careful in all the deals.
(在商場上，所有買賣都得小心。)

Julie: You are right. If your business fails, it will be very hard to make a comeback.
(你說得對。你的生意若是倒了，要東山再起會很困難。)

【相關語彙】

▸ **fail:** 失敗。fail in business 是生意倒了。

例 The business won't fail. I am sure it has hit bottom and will make a comeback.
(生意不會倒。我確定已經跌到谷底，就要開始回復了。)

▸ **a deal:** 一樁買賣；交易；契約。

例 It's a deal.
(一言為定。)

It's a good deal.
(一樁好買賣。)

【情況會話 **3**】　*********************

(兒子大學聯考沒考上。)

Mother:　Don't feel too bad. Put yourself together and make a comeback.
（不要太難過。振作起來，東山再起。）

Son:　I will, Mom. I'll study harder and make it next year.
（我會的，媽。我要更認真讀書，明年一定要成功。）

【相關語彙】

▶ **feel bad:** 覺得難過。

例 I feel very bad that Frank was canned today.
（法蘭克今天丟了工作，我很難過。）

▶ **put oneself together:** 振作起來。

例 No matter how hard it is, put yourself together and go for it.
（不論工作多困難。你自己振作起來，全力以赴。）

國家圖書館出版品預行編目資料

美國口語一週通/施孝昌, Charles Krohn 合著. --
新北市：哈福企業有限公司，2022.01
面；　公分 . --（英語系列；76）
ISBN 978-626-95576-1-5（平裝附光碟片）
1.CST: 英語 2.CST: 口語 3.CST: 會話
805.188　　　　　　　　　110022254

英語系列：76

....

書名/美國口語一週通
作者/施孝昌・Charles Krohn
出版單位/哈福企業有限公司
責任編輯/Jocelyn Chang
封面設計/李秀英
內文排版/八十文創
出版者/哈福企業有限公司
地址/新北市板橋區五權街 16 號 1 樓
電話／(02) 2808-4587 傳真／(02) 2808-6545
郵政劃撥／31598840 戶名/哈福企業有限公司
出版日期／2022 年 1 月
定價／NT$ 330 元（附 MP3）
港幣定價／110 元（附 MP3）
封面內文圖／取材自 Shutterstock

....

全球華文國際市場總代理／采舍國際有限公司
地址／新北市中和區中山路 2 段 366 巷 10 號 3 樓
電話／(02) 8245-8786 傳真／(02) 8245-8718
網址／www.silkbook.com 新絲路華文網

....

香港澳門總經銷／和平圖書有限公司
地址／香港柴灣嘉業街 12 號百樂門大廈 17 樓
電話／(852) 2804-6687 傳真／(852) 2804-6409

....

email ／ welike8686@Gmail.com
網址／ Haa-net.com
facebook ／ Haa-net 哈福網路商城

....

Original Copyright © 3S Culture Co., Ltd.

....

電子書格式：PDF